SWEET-TALKING COWBEAR

LIV BRYWOOD

Sweet-Talking Cowbear
Copyright© 2020 Liv Brywood
All rights reserved

No part of this book may be reproduced in any form or by any electronic or mechanical means including information storage and retrieval systems, without permission in writing from the author. The only exception is by a reviewer, who may quote short excerpts in a review.

This book is a work of fiction. Names, characters, places, and incidents either are products of the author's imagination or are used fictitiously. Any resemblance to actual persons, living or dead, events, or locales is entirely coincidental.

❀ Created with Vellum

1

Amber shoved her oven mitts on and raced to save a tray of gingerbread men from burning. She'd spent the last three hours in her bakery, frantically trying to fill Christmas orders before the courier arrived. It was going to be close, but once the cookies cooled, she'd be able to complete the last gift basket. The thirty-basket order wasn't unusual, but she'd been short-staffed since her employee had quit to move back home.

"I can do this," she murmured. "I'm the cookie master."

She sure didn't feel like the master of anything, but with orders piled high, she had to get them filled. There were only fifteen more days until Christmas.

She would get everything done, even if it meant riding a sugar high the entire time. She just had to focus.

An hour later, the gingerbread men were cool enough to add to the baskets. Before adding the final treat, she repositioned the snowmen and reindeer cookies she'd baked earlier in the day. As she wrapped the variety basket, the sound of crinkling cellophane filled the cinnamon and clove-scented air.

If she hadn't been in such a rush, she would have slowed down to second guess the look of every basket, but there wasn't any time. She never seemed to have enough time to get anything done these days. She seriously needed another employee, but who could she find this close to Christmas?

The bell on the bakery's front door jingled. She wiped her hands on her Santa Claus apron and walked into the restaurant section of the bakery. A woman in her late twenties with black hair and ghostly pale skin stood just inside the door next to the coat rack. Her blue eyes darted from Amber to the "Employee Wanted" sign in the window before dropping to study the floor.

"I heard you were looking for a worker. Do you have a job application form?" she whispered so softly Amber had to strain to hear.

"Yes, I'm still looking." Amber pulled a paper application out from under the counter. "Here you go."

As she held it out, the woman took a tentative step closer. "I don't really have much experience with baking, but I'm smart. I'm a quick learner."

"Go ahead and fill it out. I can't look at it right away, but I'll get back to you within a day or so." Amber handed her a pen. A buzzer went off in the kitchen. "I'll be right back."

She hurried into the kitchen to pull a batch of peanut butter blossoms out of the oven. If she didn't get the chocolate kisses pressed in fast enough, the cookies wouldn't set correctly.

After tearing open a bag of the chocolates, she pressed one into the center of each cookie. Granulated sugar sparkled like snow across the perfectly baked dough. This time she did take a second to admire them. It was her favorite holiday cookie. She could remember making them with her mother when she was a child. Sure, decorating sugar cookies was fun too, but these always held a special place in her heart.

The bell jingled, and the sound of the door closing drew her back to the front counter. The application lay on the white Formica. She glanced at it and frowned. The phone number section was blank.

She ran outside, only to be blinded by the dazzling

December sun. Shading her eyes with her hand, she spotted the woman getting into a beat-up Ford truck, circa the 1980s. Brown paint peeled around the edges. A bungee cord kept the bumper from falling off. Barely. And the vehicle coughed and sputtered as the woman turned the ignition.

"Wait!"

Amber knocked on the window. The woman jumped before rolling down the glass. Her eyes were wide, like a startled deer who'd spotted a hunter.

"You didn't leave your number."

"Oh, yeah. I don't have one yet." Pink splotches colored her cheeks. "But I can come back tomorrow if that's okay. I might have a number by then."

"Don't you have a cell phone?" Amber asked. She glanced at the application again. Her name was Raven.

"Mine... I, uh, left it at a truck stop by accident. I'm getting a new one tomorrow." Raven hung her head, and several locks of black hair fell across her eyes.

"Okay. Come by tomorrow. I just need to call to check references."

"Some of those companies went out of business. You might not be able to reach anyone."

"As long as I can get ahold of someone, it should be fine." Amber hated admitting her desperation, but she really needed help.

"Thanks." Raven rolled up the window before pulling out onto Main Street.

Amber stood on the sidewalk, watching her go. A strange woman, but beggars couldn't be choosers. As long as she could verify something about this person, Amber would hire her. She didn't have much of a choice.

When she returned to the bakery, she started in on a new batch of sweets. She measured the ingredients for chocolate cookies stuffed with peppermint into one of her stand mixers and put it to work. The scent of peppermint and chocolate hit the air instantly. She inhaled, loving the way it blended with the other smells.

"I really should enjoy this," she said. "I've got a ton of orders. Business is great. I'll get it done."

While she waited for the dough to form, she pulled the job application out of her pocket. She glanced at the information. Two old employers were listed, but her address line was blank. Super weird. Had she just moved into town?

After putting the cookies into the oven, she called the number listed next to Raven's last employer. She got a busy signal. Weird. Didn't everyone have call waiting these days?

The next number was a dead end too. It had been

disconnected. Which happened, but it still made Amber uneasy. Sure, she was desperate for help, but desperate enough to risk giving someone she didn't know the keys to the bakery? If she'd had other applications, she'd choose someone else. But she didn't.

"Where's our favorite girl?" a low, sexy voice called from the doorway to the kitchen.

Her heart fluttered when she spotted Shane. At 6'3", he was the hottest cowboy she'd ever met in Huckleberry Valley. His smile melted a soft, warm place she'd long neglected. His perpetual five-o-clock shadow, spring-green eyes, and adorable dimple stole her breath every time he walked into a room. He also happened to be her best friend, so she struggled not to glance at the bulge in his tight jeans. He wore a blue plaid, long-sleeved shirt, but no jacket. He was a bear shifter who never got cold, unlike her.

I don't get cold, her inner bear grumbled.

Shh! she silently warned the beast.

"Mommy!" Joey, Amber's seven-year-old son, came out from behind Shane's legs. "Can I have a cookie? I want a cookie. Can I? Can I?"

"Okay." She laughed. "But only one. I don't want you spoiling your lunch."

"What's on the menu?" Shane asked.

"Um," she stammered as her nipples tightened. "Peanut butter and jelly sandwiches?"

"Is that a question or a request?" Shane asked in that sultry tone that made her wonder if he was flirting with her.

"I'm sorry. I'm so backed up with cookie orders, I haven't had time to even think about lunch." She waved her hand around the kitchen. "I still have ten orders to fill today and the dishes are piling up and—"

"Hey." Shane gently grasped her shoulders. "Look at me."

She did, and instantly regretted it. The steamy look in his eyes unnerved her. He looked like he wanted to eat her for lunch, which was impossible. They'd never been romantic. In fact, he'd seemed to do everything in his power not to touch her like that.

"I'll take care of lunch," he said.

"Okay. I mean, thank you. I feel like a terrible mother for forgetting." She glanced at Joey, who was stuffing a gingerbread cookie into his little mouth. He seemed oblivious to their conversation.

"How many times do I have to tell you? You're not a bad mother. You're working your butt off, and you need help. Let me get Joey fed, then I'll pitch in until the orders are done."

"Are you sure?"

"I'm off for the next two days before I do another twenty-four-hour shift. The life of a paramedic." He chuckled as he lifted a clean apron off a hook and pulled it over his head. He tied it at the waist. Not for the first time, she wondered what he'd look like wearing *only* an apron.

"How was yesterday?" she asked.

"Discouraging." He sighed. "Last night we had two calls in the trailer park. Meth overdoses. One made it. The other didn't. It just... sucks."

"I'm sorry." She gently rubbed his upper arm. "It must be hard to see that, day in and day out."

"Most of the time, I love my job. I've helped save a lot of people. I don't mind the calls for things like heart attacks, strokes, lacerations, but it's those drug calls..." He shook his head. "It's the same people too. I've saved them over and over, but they don't stop. Even with interventions. Even with treatment."

"A few must get clean, right?"

"Some. But I never get to see those cases. Just the bad ones. It skews things." He rolled his shoulders and stretched his neck from side to side. "Anyway, enough about that. Let me get lunch done, then I'll help you with your cookies."

She didn't trust herself to answer, because every dirty thought she'd managed to push down came rushing back up. Shane. Naked. With only an apron on. It wasn't fair that her mind tormented her like this.

Maybe he's our mate, her bear suggested.

She laughed out loud.

"What's so funny?" Joey asked, crumbs dropping from his chipmunk cheeks.

"Nothing." But when she glanced up at Shane, he was studying her in a way that suggested he might be undressing her with his eyes. Naughty.

She dragged her attention back to the cookie list for the next order. She didn't trust herself to look up at him again. He was the worst kind of temptation. The one she definitely couldn't have. She relied on him to help with Joey. Shane spent hours and hours babysitting—without pay—because he was a good guy. The best. And she couldn't mess that up. So, no matter how much she wanted to lick him like a spatula covered with cream cheese frosting, she couldn't. He was her best friend. Nothing more. And it would have to stay that way.

Shane stole glances at Amber. She was gorgeous, as usual. How any man could have left her was beyond him. Her ex-husband was a fool. Her eyes held so much anguish from everything she'd had to endure after the divorce. Shane wanted to fly to New York City and kick her ex's ass, but he'd never be that foolish.

As she moved around the bakery, the sway of her curvy hips and plump bottom drew his gaze. He had to be quick to look away so she wouldn't catch him, but it was worth the risk. Her stunning green eyes, long red hair, and pale skin made her Irish descent obvious. She wore her hair up in a bun covered with a hairnet when she was baking, but his fingers itched to pull it free and watch her curly locks cascade down her naked back.

There you go again, his bear silently communicated. *Drooling all over our mate. Why don't you just ask her out? Or whatever you silly humans do. You should just mate with her and find out if she's the one.*

I wish it were that simple, he told his bear.

Why isn't it?

She's skittish. Her marriage imploded, and she's afraid to even date now. Her ex did a real number on her.

So, fix it, his bear demanded.

He sighed. If only it were that easy. Women were complicated. Just when he thought he had one figured out, they'd up and change on him. His friendship with Amber was steady. Stable. Predictable. And with a job as chaotic as his could be, he craved consistency. With

Amber, he knew exactly what he was getting. To mess that up would be stupid.

You do dumb stuff all the time, like run into dangerous situations to save people. Remember that coked-out dude with the green mohawk and gold teeth? You still saved his kid who'd fallen into a diabetic coma, his bear said.

True.

How is this any different? As if to make his point, his bear swiped his claws across Shane's ribcage.

"Ouch!" Shane gasped and grabbed his stomach.

"Are you that hungry?" Amber teased. "Eat one of my cookies."

Desire rushed through his veins, even though he knew she wasn't talking about *that* cookie.

"I'll help make sandwiches," Joey declared.

He was only tall enough to be chin-height with the prep table, but he was just as determined as his mother to accomplish his tasks. He was Amber's mini-me, and Shane hoped that one day he could have a son as precocious and sweet as Joey. He'd always wanted to be a father. One day he'd find the right woman, and they'd start a family together. Or, who knew, maybe she'd come with a ready-made family from a previous relationship, like Amber did. Dating a single mom didn't scare him. If anything, it made him admire her so much more. It had to be hard, doing everything alone.

Shane pulled bread off a shelf and grabbed the jars of peanut butter and jelly. After setting everything on the counter, he took out three plates.

"Do you want to do the peanut butter or the jelly?" he asked.

"Jelly!" Joey yelled.

"Inside voice," Amber said.

"Sorry, Mom."

"It's okay. I'm glad I decided to keep the restaurant closed today. I've had a couple of disappointed phone calls, but everyone understands that I'm short staffed." She kneaded a pile of sticky dough with her strong, sexy hands.

"Any luck on hiring someone new?" He hated that she had to look for help. He wanted to be there for her, but he had a demanding job. Just one more reason why he couldn't be with her.

"I got an application."

"Just one?" He frowned as he spread peanut butter across three pieces of bread.

"It's almost Christmas. No one's looking for work."

"Who was it? Someone from town?"

"I don't think so. Her name's Raven. Maybe you've seen her around? She's in her late 20s, black hair, but I think it's dyed. Really pale skin. Blue eyes. Ring a bell?"

"Not really. I don't remember anyone like that around here."

"She didn't put down an address, so I'm not sure if she just moved here or what's going on."

"No address?" He set the knife on the counter. "That's strange."

"That wasn't the only weird thing. No phone number either. And when I tried to check references, I couldn't get through to anyone."

"I know you're desperate for help, but these are all red flags."

"What's a red flag?" Joey asked.

Shane squatted down until he was eye level with the boy. "You know that feeling you get when you know something's not right?"

"Like when Mom orders salad instead of pizza?" Joey glanced at his mom, a slight frown on his little face.

"Something like that." Shane grinned at Amber. "It just means we have to be careful."

"Like not talking to strangers?" Joey cocked his head.

"Exactly! You should never talk to anyone you don't know." Shane riffled Joey's hair. "Are you almost done with the jelly?"

Joey had managed to get it on the bread, as well as his face, hands, and in his hair.

"Yep!"

"Perfect. Go wash your hands, and we can sit together."

"Oh, I really don't have time," Amber said.

"Five minutes." Shane flashed a smile. "Then I'll help you, and we'll knock out your orders. By the way, how many do you have?"

"Eight more."

"Piece of cake."

Amber groaned while Shane smirked at his silly joke.

"The orders are for one hundred cookies each." She raised a brow.

"How many can you fit in the oven at a time?" He glanced at the appliance with skepticism.

"Not enough. I really need another. Maybe two. But there's no space. And I can't afford to move the shop. Between the rent and the insurance, I'm doing okay, but not well enough to expand."

"Maybe one day."

"Maybe." She gave him a tired smile as she sat on the stool next to him. Their knees touched for a brief moment, sending sparks skittering through his body.

Sweet-Talking Cowbear

Just sitting this close to her was enough to make him painfully hard.

"Have you baked cookies before?" she asked before taking a bite of her sandwich.

"With my grandmother, yes. She had us lined up like a sweatshop. I think she baked ten thousand cookies every year. Enough for every church function as well as Huckleberry Valley's Annual Christmas Party. It's a good thing they pushed it back a week this year. They moved it to Saturday the 19th so people wouldn't have to choose between Melody and Wyatt's wedding and the Christmas party. My grandmother will probably need a whole table for her baked goods by then." He laughed.

"I have four orders due that day. It's five days away, but I still have other orders before those." Her tone went from calm to frazzled by the time she'd finished speaking.

"Sweetie, we're going to get it done. I've got to work tomorrow, then I'm all yours."

Sweetie? All yours? His bear chuffed silently.

Okay, wrong choice of words, he told his bear.

Or exactly right. His bear grinned.

"You're a lifesaver." She gazed at him as if he were the most important man in the world. "How can I ever repay you for everything you've done for me?"

"Go to the Annual Christmas Party with me," he blurted.

"I have so much to do."

"You can take a few hours off. Can't you?" He covered her hand with his.

She turned hers and held on. "It's at night, right?"

"Starts at five."

"The bakery will be closed by then. I guess I could spend a few hours there."

"Good. I'll pick you up from here. I'll already have Joey since I promised to babysit this weekend."

"Sometimes I think you're too good to be true."

"All the ladies tell me that." He waggled his eyebrows. She burst out laughing, which was music to his ears. Seeing the joy on her face gave him an enormous amount of satisfaction. She deserved to be happy, and he was ready to do everything in his power to make that happen.

"Okay, master baker, where do I start?" He cleared the empty lunch plates before rolling up his sleeves.

For the next three hours, he kneaded and mixed and spooned out cookies. Joey helped with decorating, and Amber managed the whole operation. Something warm and gooey seeped into his heart. Affection, and maybe something more. But he wasn't ready to give it a name just yet.

Thinking about her as anything other than a friend was a slippery slope, and he wasn't ready to go sliding. He needed her in his life. Trying to rush into a relationship would only push her away, which was the last thing he ever wanted to do. Falling in love with her would be a total disaster. If she didn't feel the same way, then he'd ruin their friendship forever. And he wasn't ready to take that risk.

2

Amber tied a blue and white bow on the last Chanukah basket of the day. It was after six, and Joey was grumbling about being hungry. The thought of cooking after working all day made her want to die a little.

"How does Huckleberry Café sound for dinner?" she asked in as cheery a tone as she could muster.

"I could cook dinner at my house... or your house. Whatever." Shane stuffed his hands into the apron's pockets. He couldn't have looked any more adorable in that moment.

"You've already helped so much. Let me take you out. My treat. Besides, Joey's been begging me to take him there for a milkshake for days."

"Yaysss!" Joey hissed with glee. He high-fived Shane, who laughed.

"Well, I can't say no now, can I?" Shane asked in a teasing tone.

"I guess not." She grinned but wondered if maybe he didn't want to go. She'd roped him in without really asking. Although, he did offer to cook at his house... She was probably just overthinking it. Again.

After cleaning the kitchen and tossing their aprons into the laundry bin, they headed toward the front door. Through the window, she watched a swirl of snow dance across the sidewalk.

"Jackets and hats," she said. "Looks chilly outside."

"We're supposed to get a storm around midnight," Shane said.

"Cool! Can we make snowmen tomorrow?" Joey asked as he pulled on his winter coat, knit hat, and gloves.

"Of course. But it's going to have to be really early, because I have a lot of cookies to make tomorrow." Amber wound a small scarf around Joey's neck to help keep him warm.

"Am I playing here tomorrow?" Joey looked at Shane.

"I've got to work, buddy. But I'm off this weekend,

and we're going to the annual Christmas party. We can hang out then, okay?"

"Can we have hot chocolate with marshmallows?" Joey's eyes went wide.

"If your mom says it's okay." Shane winked at her.

"I don't see why not."

"Will Santa be there?" Joey asked.

"I sure hope so," Amber said.

She shot a warning look at Shane. Huckleberry Valley had a huge problem this year. For the last decade, Wallace Jackson had been playing the jolly old man. But because of his dementia, he wasn't going to be able to do it this year.

As far as she knew, they didn't have a Santa yet, but she'd been trying to cajole every older man in town to take the position. It was only for one day, but no one seemed to want to do it. She'd thought about asking Shane, but he already did so much for her, and for the other people in town. If anyone needed him, he was there. She didn't want to take advantage of him.

"Ready?" Shane asked, holding out his arm. Always the gentleman.

"Let's go." She grasped Joey's mittened hand in hers and followed Shane outside.

The sidewalk had iced over. She slipped forward,

almost pulling Joey over as she crashed into Shane. He grabbed her to steady her.

"I should have bought new snow boots for this year. Mine are a bit old," she said by way of apology.

"No worries. I got you." Shane's smile sent tendrils of desire unfurling through her belly.

"You always do, don't you?" she asked softly.

"As much as I can."

She wasn't sure what he meant by that, but she wasn't about to ask either. Instead, she hooked her arm tightly through his and held onto Joey a bit tighter. They walked into the wind. Biting snowflakes crashed into her cheeks. By the time they'd walked a block down to the café, her nose was frozen, and her eyes watered.

As soon as they were safely inside the café, she sighed with relief. Although the weather normally didn't bother her, she was exhausted and not happy about having to deal with it. She'd bitten off way more than she could chew this year. She'd only been trying to get a little bit ahead of her bills by taking extra orders, but now she wasn't sure if her plan made sense. She couldn't cancel any orders. All she could do was bring on more help.

"I'll be right with you," Gloria called from across the café. "Sit anywhere you want."

"She's been glowing ever since she married Vern," Amber said. A twinge of jealousy darkened her heart for a moment. She was happy for them, but it reminded her of her own failed marriage.

"Vern can't stop grinning either." Shane gestured toward a booth, and they piled in. Shane sat across from Joey and Amber. "I swear the man looks ten years younger."

"Don't you dare let my husband hear you say that." Gloria grinned. "He's already flying on cloud nine, and I don't need him up on ten trying to pull me up there too."

"There's a cloud ten?" Shane's eyes twinkled.

"Vern sure thinks there is. I thought I was marrying an old man. Turns out I married a man ready for his second wind. I can hardly keep up with him, and I'm on my feet four hours a day here." Gloria blew a lock of hair off her wrinkled forehead. She looked amazing for her age. Although she'd never told anyone the exact year of her birth, Amber figured she was in her sixties. "What can I get you guys?"

"A chocolate milkshake with sprinkles. Please." Joey grinned from ear to ear.

"I'd like a coffee with cream," Amber said.

"At this time of night? How will you sleep?" Shane asked.

"Trust me, I'll be fine. I'm about to fall face first into my menu." Amber shot him a wry but tired smile.

"I'll take an iced tea," Shane said.

After Gloria left to fill their order, Amber nudged Shane with her foot. In a teasing tone, she said, "That has caffeine in it, you know. You might be up until sunrise."

"Unlike some people..." He sat back and finished in a mock-snooty voice. "I can handle my stimulants."

"What else do you take to stay up all night?" she asked.

"Oh, a little of this and a little of that." He averted his eyes in an exaggerated way.

"You guys are weird," Joey said.

Shane laughed, while Amber shook her head. When his eyes met hers, a zing of awareness rippled through her body. She shifted her weight from one hip to the other and crossed her legs, accidentally bumping him in the process.

"Are you playing footsies with me?" Shane asked in a low, sexy voice.

"Gross!" Joey yelped. "Don't you know girls have cooties?"

"Are those like germs?" Shane asked while keeping his sparkling gaze on hers.

"Bad germs. You can't get rid of them. You get *inflected*." Joey nodded sagely.

"Infected. And I won't give him cooties. Not unless he wants them," she added playfully. But it wasn't just to keep the conversation lighthearted; she was also testing his reaction.

His pupils darkened, and the shadow of his bear moved just under the surface. He swallowed as he searched her face. She wasn't willing to give anything away. Instead, she plastered a smile on and acted as if she'd been perfectly innocent. But she'd seen enough to suspect he might be interested in her. More than she'd imagined.

However, interest and desire on their own didn't make for a good relationship. She'd figured that out the hard way when her ex-husband left her. At least he hadn't cheated, unless applying for a job with no intention of taking his family with him constituted cheating. Maybe it did.

"You're frowning," Shane said softly.

Amber shook off the dark thoughts. Dwelling on the past wouldn't change anything. Being present with Shane and Joey right now was far more important.

"Sorry it took a minute," Gloria said as she returned and passed out the drinks. "The ice cream machine's been having a fit all week. We're supposed to be getting a new one next spring, but that seems like a hundred years away."

"It will get here before you know it," Shane said.

"I sure hope so. What can I get you for dinner?" After taking everyone's orders, she said, "It'll be right up. Let me know if you need refills."

"Can I get one?" Joey asked.

"After you eat dinner, if you're still hungry," Amber said. It was a bargain that always worked in her favor, since her son never finished everything on his plate. Which was fine with her. Leftovers meant less cooking. Standing over a hot stove was the last thing she wanted to do after baking all day.

"Yay!" Joey slurped through his straw until his face crinkled. He gasped, "Brain freeze!"

"Take a break, buddy," Shane said. "Let your tummy catch up."

"Okay." Joey narrowed his gaze at the milkshake as if challenging it not to melt.

The corner of Shane's mouth tugged up, sending warmth spooling through her belly. No matter how much time they spent together, she couldn't seem to get past the butterflies. Just one look was enough to send her into fantasy land. And try as she might, she had to stop thinking about him that way. If she lost him as a babysitter, she'd be in a world of trouble. She felt guilty thinking about him in those terms, but it was the honest truth. She loved her son but being a single mom could really suck sometimes.

Shane's phone buzzed. He glanced at it before giving her an apologetic smile. "I'm sorry. It's my ranch manager. I have to take this. Hello?"

As he slid out of the booth, she risked a glance at his butt. Damn did he look good in denim. It had been far, far too long since she'd been with a man. Maybe that was the problem. Maybe she only wanted Shane because she'd been alone for years.

When he returned to the table, Gloria had already dropped off the food. He sat and pulled his plate closer.

"Everything okay?" Amber asked.

"Leave it up to the cows to start trouble in the dead of winter." He shook his head. "One got out, and we've been looking for her for a few days. I figured she'd fallen into a pond or something when we couldn't find her right away."

"Oh no." Amber's heart sunk.

"Oh, don't worry. She's okay. She's in with Shannon Wells' stock. The bulls, of course. Shannon's probably going to charge me a pretty penny for letting one of her guys impregnate my darn cow. I wouldn't blame her if she did. I had to give my manager a talkin' to because he left one of the gates open. That's how she escaped. He finally fessed up after I've spent the last few days trying to figure it out." He stabbed a French fry through a glob of ketchup before popping it into his mouth.

"I'm glad he found her."

"Me too." He took a sip of tea. "Maybe Shannon will let me trade my manager for the stud fee."

Amber wasn't sure if he was kidding until he smirked. She relaxed.

"Don't mind me. I just get annoyed when I'm paying him a pretty penny and he screws up," Shane said.

"Maybe you should lower his pay," she suggested.

"Nah. He's still better than most. But I've been thinking about cutting back my hours at my paramedic job."

"Why?" Amber picked up her chicken Caesar wrap and took a bite. The tangy dressing and crisp lettuce perked her up. Other than the peanut butter and jelly, she hadn't stopped to eat all day.

"Just..." Shane's jaw twitched. "I don't really need the money. I make enough with the ranch. More than enough, really."

"Why haven't you quit already?"

"I can't. Not entirely." Shane picked up his burger. "I'm just not ready to go yet."

As she worked her way through her wrap and side of potato salad, she contemplated his response. What did it mean that he wasn't ready? She'd known him for several years now and being a paramedic had seemed like his calling. But maybe he was regretting it after seeing so many drug overdoses. Still, she couldn't help but feel there was more to his story. Too bad he was holding back. She wished he'd open up to her a little more. After all, he'd called her his best friend more than once. Didn't best friends share everything?

Shane didn't want to tell her the real reason he couldn't stop working as a paramedic. They'd always kept their relationship light and fun. She was the one person he could be completely himself with, and he didn't want to wreck things by revealing his darkest secret. But a part of him wanted to tell her anyway. She wouldn't judge. She never had a bad word about anyone, except her ex who definitely deserved it.

"Are the rest of the cows okay?" Amber asked.

"Yep. I'm running a hundred head at the moment. After all these years, I have the whole place working like a well-oiled machine. Well, as long as my ranch manager isn't screwing things up. If beef prices hold up next spring, I might even be able to add to the herd. But you never know with the economy, so we'll see."

"If you did retire from being a paramedic, what would you do all day? I mean, I know ranching's a ton of work, but wouldn't you get lonely?" she asked.

"Ranching is anything but boring." He chuckled. "The minute you make a dent in your to-do list, five more things get added on. It's never-ending."

"I know what you mean." She sat back and sighed. Her sweater pulled tight across her breasts, and it took extreme willpower to look away. He wanted to touch her but had to settle for the last bite of his burger instead.

"How many orders do you have tomorrow?" he asked.

"I think I only have five. But they're smaller than today. The bakery's open tomorrow too, so I have to deal with customers. I'm going to try to verify the woman's employment history, but I've got to be honest. I need help; I might just hire her out of desperation." Worry furrowed her brow.

"You could always fingerprint her and ask the sheriff to run them. Make sure she's not a criminal."

"True."

"Or, if you can get her social security number,

you can run a background check. Try a little Googling to see if you can find out anything about her. Everyone has an online presence. Social media. Old addresses. I'm sure you'll come up with something. But if you're worried about it, maybe you can get someone from the café to work a shift. Maybe one of the ladies would like extra Christmas money." He lifted his cup and pointed it toward one of the servers.

"I guess it wouldn't hurt to ask."

"Gloria." He motioned her over.

"Need a refill?" Gloria asked when she reached the table.

"Actually, I was wondering if you were busy tomorrow," Amber said. "I need some help in the bakery. I can pay you. I'm just up to my eyeballs in orders and since I lost my employee, I'm starting to get overwhelmed."

"Oh, hon. I wish I could, but I promised Vern we'd go over to Wyatt and Melody's place to help them hang decorations. It's a family tradition. Well, we're starting it anyway. Didn't use to do it in the past, but this year's different. So many things have changed." Gloria's eyes shimmered as she smiled. "Also, Vern wants to measure the baby's room so he can get started on nursery furniture. Melody's going to have the baby in June, but I don't want him waiting until the last minute to get the crib done."

"That is so sweet of Vern," Amber said.

"Let me ask some of the other girls and see if anyone's free," Gloria said. "Dessert?"

Joey's head whipped up from his half-eaten plate of chicken nuggets.

"You already drank your dessert," Amber told him. "Shane?"

"I'm stuffed. But I could go for some coffee." He didn't want to leave until Gloria had a chance to ask the others if they could help Amber. He hated seeing the look of desperation in her face. If he wasn't working so much, he'd be able to help more. But then he'd have to walk away from saving people. What if someone died because he wasn't there?

"Coffee at this hour?" Amber teased.

"Maybe you should lock me in the bakery all night and put me to work." He leaned forward.

"Not a bad idea." She tugged at the edge of her bottom lip with her teeth. A low growl of desire rumbled through his chest. Her eyes widened, and she released her lip.

"Must have been something I ate." His cheeks burned.

"Must have been." She clearly didn't believe him at

all, but she didn't seem revolted either. If anything, confusion flickered in her eyes.

Didn't she know how beautiful she was? God, he wanted to tell her, but he couldn't. If only she wasn't his best friend. If only she were a complete stranger. Then he'd be able to act on his longing. He wouldn't have to hold back and pretend that keeping his hands to himself wasn't pure torture. All he'd ever wanted to do was pull her into his arms and kiss her breathless. His bear dared him to do it at least once a week, but he hadn't given in to the temptation. And he never would. He'd never ruin their friendship just to satisfy his lust.

And then there was Joey to think about. Shane knew he had no right to pretend Joey was his son, but part of him wanted to. He loved the kid. While Amber worked, they'd gone out and played soccer together. On other occasions, Shane had tossed baseballs for Joey to hit. Hell, Shane had taken a baseball to the nuts without complaint.

Maybe his desire to have a family was making him crazy, but he already kind of thought about them as his family. If Amber ever found out, he had no idea what she'd do. She'd probably be horrified. They weren't supposed to be family, only friends. But then again, unless he blurted something out, she'd never know his true feelings. It was better that way.

"Well, hon. It's not looking good." Gloria returned with her hands on her hips. "Everyone's busy. I even offered to chip in to pay a little extra so they could help you, but they're all either working here, or at their other jobs, or they just can't do it for some other reason. Sorry."

"Thanks for asking around," Amber said.

Although she tried not to look dejected, Shane noted the slump in her shoulders and the shadows under her eyes. She was exhausted and needed help. Somehow, he'd have to figure out a way to get extra helpers to the bakery tomorrow.

An idea sparked. He smiled. If he could pull it off, she wouldn't have to worry about being alone. He might not be able to help her himself, but he knew whom he could ask.

"Ready to head home?" Amber asked.

"Sure." He pulled out his wallet.

"Oh, you don't have to do that. I said I'd take care of it," Amber protested.

"It's my pleasure." When she tried to push his wallet back toward him, he chuckled. "Seriously. I've got it."

"You're too good to us." Amber smiled.

"Just save me a few cookies for later in the week." He winked. When she blushed, his heart skipped a few beats.

You're in love with her, his bear silently communicated.

He ignored his bear. Now wasn't the time for a debate, but deep down, he knew the beast might be right. He couldn't acknowledge it though. That would just be asking for trouble. Instead, he pushed the thought aside.

As they headed toward the door, he placed a hand on Amber's lower back. He grasped Joey's small hand in his and together, they walked out into the snowy winter night.

When they stopped at Amber's truck, she helped Joey inside. She shut the door before turning to Shane.

"Thanks again for dinner. Next time it's my treat, okay?" She stood on her tiptoes and brushed a soft kiss across his cheek.

His heart leapt into his throat. Unable to reply, he simply nodded.

"See you in a few days." She got into the truck.

The sound of the door closing snapped him out of his trance. She'd kissed him. Holy hell. But, as a friend, right? He waited until she drove off before reaching up to touch his cheek. It had to have been a kiss of gratitude, nothing else. The kind of kiss friends gave each other after dinner...

Who was he kidding? Friends didn't usually kiss each other after dinner. Did they? Had he ever kissed a friend after dinner? Hell no!

A grin spread across his face. She'd freakin' kissed him.

"Hell yeah." He jumped and fist-pumped the air.

Maybe it didn't mean anything, but he didn't care. He'd worry about that later. For now, he'd continue to savor the phantom feel of her lips on his cheek until he couldn't remember the sensation anymore. Which might never happen. But if it did, maybe he'd just have to find a way to get her to kiss him again.

3

Shane smiled as the headlights on his truck cut through the darkness to illuminate the gravel road leading up the hill to his grandmother's house. He'd offered to pave it for her, but she'd refused, telling him that bouncing along it was the only action she'd been able to get since her husband, his grandfather, had passed. That had been three years ago. She still hadn't changed her mind, but he made it a point of asking her about it every winter. He didn't like thinking about her driving down the road on a dark, snowy, winter night. Maybe he'd work harder this year to convince her to let him pave it.

Light shined out of the old farmhouse's living room window. His grandmother always got up by five a.m. to do her Tai Chi. As he parked near the front door, he spotted her moving gracefully through her routine. Instead of bothering her by ringing the doorbell, he waved through the window before heading inside. She still didn't lock her door, despite his insistence that she do so. The world wasn't as safe anymore, and although she lived up a hill in the middle of nowhere, one never knew when some desperate person with ill intention would show up. At least she kept a shotgun by the door.

"Tea kettle is in the kitchen," she called. "I'll be done in a minute."

"Sounds good, Grandma."

He found her heavy gauge, copper teapot on the stove. He grabbed it and filled it with water from the sink. The etched floral bamboo pattern glistened in the light. He turned on the stove and, after two clicks, flames whooshed up from the gas. He turned the nob down then set the pot over it.

"Want breakfast?" he asked.

"Just some toast and jam for me."

As he set about making her breakfast, he hummed to himself. He still couldn't believe Amber had kissed him. Not on the mouth, of course, but close enough.

"You look cheery." His grandmother walked into the kitchen with the grace of a dancer. "Who's the lucky girl?"

"What?" He flushed.

How did she *do* that? She'd always been able to look at him and guess what he was thinking, more or less.

"Okay, don't tell me." She chuckled. "I can guess who it is anyway."

"What do you mean?" he asked.

"Amber." She smirked as she took the plate of toast from him. "Come sit down."

He sat at the oak table. "I can't stay too long. I need to be at work at six."

"Well then, out with it." She slathered homemade huckleberry jam onto the toast before taking a bite.

"It is about Amber," he admitted.

"Knew it."

"I really hate to ask, but she needs help baking today, and I know you like to bake."

"*Like* to bake?" She balanced her toast on the edge of her plate. "I *live* to bake! What's going on?"

"She has a bunch of Christmas orders to fill, and the store's open tomorrow. Her only employee left, and she really needs help. She can't keep the shop closed while she bakes. I'd help her, but I start a twenty-four-hour shift today."

"What about Joey?"

"He's going to have to sit at the bakery all day

unless Amber can get her mother to babysit. Lately, Blythe hasn't offered to watch Joey as much as she used to. I think she enjoys watching Amber struggle."

"That woman." His grandmother rolled her eyes. "If I had the chance to have my grandbabies with me, I'd never let them go. What do you think she needs the most help with Joey or the store?"

"I'm really not sure."

"Pfft," she waved away the question. "Doesn't matter. I just need to shower and I'm heading down there."

"At least wait until daylight," he pleaded.

She turned to look out the window, squinting. "By the time I get ready it will be sunrise. Good enough for me. Now, I've got you for thirty more minutes, right?"

"I'm all yours." He grinned.

"Good. Because I've got this idea." She leaned back and folded her age-spotted arms over her yellow yoga top.

"Oh no." He shook his head. "I can already tell I'm not going to like whatever you're about to say."

"I want to open a Tai Chi place for seniors. There's enough of us in the valley, and I'm sick of seeing everyone hobbling around with their canes and walkers. Old man Newsom almost tripped me up with his cane the other day."

"On purpose?" He sat up.

"Nah." She huffed. "Senility or stupidity. Not sure which. Anyway, remember my old neighbor Jinjing?"

"We used to go to tea at her house when I was a kid."

"I'm surprised you remember that."

"Her house had such unusual Chinese decorations. And she had cool toys for me to play with," he said.

"She was a good woman. I visited her at least once a week until last year when the lung cancer finally got her. I tried to get her to quit smoking, but she refused. Claimed it kept her young. Hogwash. It was the Tai Chi." She tapped her finger on the table for emphasis.

"It's too bad about the cancer."

"A terrible way to go." She clucked her tongue. "Anyway, I don't know if I ever told you much about her, but her family moved her in 1882. We weren't even a state yet. Back then it was Montana Territory."

"I remember." He sat back, knowing she was about to go into another one of her stories. He never minded listening, but he hoped she'd get to the point before he had to leave. He didn't want to have to cut her off before she was done.

"They came over from China to work on the Bozeman pass in 1882. It was part of the Northern

Pacific Railway," she added. "You did a book report about that, right?"

"Yep. It was part of a science report on geology."

"Well, her family helped build it. They lived in Bozeman at the time, but in 1882, President Chester Arthur signed the Chinese Exclusion Act. See, back then people were racist as hell against the Chinese. They didn't want them coming in and taking up all the railroad jobs.

"Her parents were scared and fled to Huckleberry Valley. They started up the ranch next door, and they've been on that land ever since. Her damn kids put it up for sale. Can you believe that? Over one hundred years in the family, and now they're selling. It's shameful what they're doing."

"Grandma, that's super interesting, but I have to get going soon."

"The reason I bring all this up is because she taught me all the Tai Chi she knew. Eventually, I looked on the YouTube and found out about moves she didn't know. I'm all educated now on it, and I want to start a business."

"Businesses are a ton of work. In some bigger cities, people do Tai Chi in the park. It's not formal. Anyone can show up. And different people take turns leading the group."

"Hum." She tapped her nails on the table. "That's an interesting idea. I called the county to find out how to get a business going, and it was a mess of paperwork. This sounds a lot easier."

"It would be. And I'm sure everyone in Huckleberry Valley, young and older, would love it."

"I could probably teach some of the youngsters," she mused. "Maybe Amber would want to join in too. I'd still be up at five in the morning. That way people could get some movement in before work."

"That sounds like a plan." He pushed back from the table. "I've got to go, Grandma. But I'll see you at the Huckleberry Valley Annual Christmas Party on Saturday."

"I've been looking forward to it all month." She stood and walked him to the door. "Thanks for coming by. I'm happy to help Amber out. She's going to be my granddaughter-in-law someday."

"What?" His belly clenched as if he'd been punched.

"Oh, don't play dumb with me, boy. I've seen the way you moon over her whenever she's around. Why haven't you asked the girl out?"

"She's my best friend," he said lamely.

"Exactly. Why wouldn't you marry her? Your granddaddy was my best friend too. I think we always knew we'd end up together." She smiled, but tears glistened in her eyes. "God rest his soul."

"I don't want to do anything to ruin our friendship," he said softly.

"Ppft!" She waved away his concern. "Life's too damn short for worrying about stupid stuff. She's a cutie and comes ready made with a great-grandson. It's inevitable, just like that bald, crazy looking guy in that movie."

He cocked his head to one side. "Who?"

"You know, the big, ugly superhero movie guy. He snaps his fingers—" She snapped hers. "—and poof! Bye bye half of the universe."

"I don't think I've seen that one."

"You work too much. Give grandma a kiss." She stretched up and turned her cheek. He gave her a quick peck. "Don't you worry. I'll take care of Amber and Joey."

"Thank you." He gave her a hug.

"Okay, gone with you." She herded him out the door. "I've got to get ready. I wonder if she needs extra baking sheets."

As his grandmother muttered under her breath about what to take to the bakery, he headed toward his truck. Even though he couldn't be there in person to help Amber, his grandmother could. He wouldn't have asked her, but he knew how much she loved baking, so it made sense. With that sorted, he headed down the snowy road toward the heart of Huckleberry Valley.

AMBER GLANCED at the clock on the wall. It was five a.m. She had exactly one hour until the bakery opened. Just enough time to swap the croissants out and slide the trays for the first cookie order into the oven. It was going to be tight, because she'd had to bake everything for the bakery customers before the store opened. Between serving people and filling the orders, she didn't know how she was going to keep her head screwed on.

Coffee. Coffee was how.

She grabbed the biggest mug she had and filled it with steaming coffee before dropping two tablespoons of brown sugar in. She added pure cream and stirred. Screw calories. She needed the sugar to get moving.

Thoroughly amped up and ready to rock, she tightened her apron before going out to unlock the front door. Three customers were standing outside, looking like human popsicles. She felt terrible about not checking earlier to make sure no one was waiting, but she'd been too busy to look.

"Come on in. I've got a fresh pot of coffee brewing."

Two of her older male customers sat at the lunch counter bar on cotton-candy pink gumdrop-shaped stools. She brought them one black coffee and one with two creamer cups and two sugar packets.

"Cinnamon rolls?" she asked.

"Always," one of the men said with a smile. The other grunted. He never did say much but was a good listener to his friend who liked to talk almost nonstop.

She found the other customer, a woman who worked at the hardware store, sitting in a booth.

"Morning! What can I get you?" Amber asked.

"Anything to help with a hangover," she grumbled.

"Rough night?"

"Too much eggnog. Gosh, I love the stuff. But it sure doesn't like me." She gave Amber a weak smile.

"I've got just the thing." She headed into the kitchen and grabbed a couple of cream puffs and an extra-large cup of coffee.

When she brought it back to the table, the woman grinned. "Well, things are certainly looking up."

"Cream or sugar?" Amber asked.

"Black's fine. There's probably enough cream and sugar in this pastry to soften up the coffee."

"You'd be surprised by how much I can cram in there." Amber chuckled.

"Don't tell me. Let me enjoy it without the guilt."

Amber smiled as she headed toward a new group of customers. The morning rush was in full swing. She raced between tables and the kitchen. Several businessmen from in town were deep in conversation by the time she made it over to take their order. She caught bits and pieces of the conversation. It sounded like things were going well, which was good for the overall economy. She certainly couldn't complain. She could hardly fill all the orders she was getting.

After handling the pre-work crowd, she took a moment to stop and make another batch of cookies. Someone rang the bell on the front counter just as she was rolling out the dough. She wiped her hands on her apron and went to see what they needed.

"Grandma Rose!" Amber's heart swelled as she spotted the sweet older lady. "What are you doing out so early?"

"Ppft! I'm up before dawn every day. Heard you needed help, so I'm here to do whatever I can. Just point me to your flour, and I'll get right on things."

"Oh, I don't really—"

"Now, don't go wasting my time. I've got things to do later, but I'm here now. Put me to work," Rose said.

"Are you sure?" Amber eyed the elderly woman who could probably still run circles around her.

"Let's get going." Rose walked around the counter. She already had a yellow and black apron on, which made her look like a bumble bee. She buzzed into the kitchen, and Amber shook her head. This had to be Shane's idea. It was sweet of him to send her, but sometimes Grandma Rose could be exhausting.

Amber followed her into the kitchen section of the bakery.

"What's next on the list?" Rose asked. She plucked an order sheet off the counter and studied it.

Amber pointed out the next item. "Gingerbread orange scones."

"Hum. Never made those before. Got a recipe?"

"Right here." Amber pulled her cookbook off a shelf. She had all the recipes memorized but didn't have time to rattle off the ingredients to Rose. "Thank you so much. You don't know what this means to me."

"It's a pleasure to help. I can only pawn off so many cookies to the girls at Bingo, and I still have the baking bug. It won't fly away until after Christmas. Now, if I had a lot of great grandbabies to feed, then I'd have a reason to stay in the kitchen."

Amber wasn't sure if Rose was narrowing her eyes because she was trying to imply something or not. She wasn't sure what to make of the sudden whirlwind of activity. She was grateful for the extra set of hands but hoped it wouldn't come with any strings attached. Grandma Rose had a way of getting her to agree with things she didn't really want to do. Amber just couldn't say 'no' to her.

"Where's Joey?" Rose asked.

"He's with my mom until noon." She grimaced, thinking about the argument she'd had with her mother that morning. Her mom just couldn't let go of the fact that Amber was a single mom. She didn't think it was natural for a woman to be on her own with a child. But what choice did Amber have? Her jerk of an ex had left her with Joey when he divorced her. Which was better anyway because she never would have agreed to joint custody. She couldn't trust Fred to keep their son safe.

"When he shows up, I'll be happy to take him for the rest of the day," Rose said.

"I thought you said you have something else you need to do."

"Feeding the ducks at the park is the other thing, but I'll take Joey along if you want. He loves those little quackers."

"Quackers?"

"Quack! Quack!" Rose waddled in a silly imitation of a duck. "He loves it."

"I'd feel so bad having you work all morning here and then having you spend all afternoon watching him." Amber reached behind herself to rub her already aching back.

"Not any trouble," Rose assured her. "Where are the spices?"

"Over here." She showed her where to find all the ingredients she'd need for the scones. "I have to run out and check on the customers."

"Don't worry. I won't burn this place down while you're gone." Rose gave her as wicked a grin as any sweet old grandmother could manage.

Laughing but shocked at her luck, Amber relaxed for the first time that day. She was able to slow her pace and take time to talk to her customers. It was something she loved to do. So many people were lonely, and she wanted everyone to know that she cared about them. Even if it was just as an acquaintance. People needed to be seen and heard, and she intended to do that as much as she could.

A little after noon, she caught a whiff of something acrid. Smoke? She ran into the kitchen to find Rose throwing a tray of charred cookies into the sink.

"Forgot to set the timer on that one," Rose said, apologetically.

"Don't worry. I've done it more times than I can count. Are you okay? You didn't get burnt, did you?"

"Nah." She held up oven mitts shaped like huge bear paws. "These babies kept me safe."

"You've been working for hours. Why don't you take a break and have something to eat?" Amber suggested.

"Had my morning toast. Nothing more until dinner. I don't get hungry during the day. Also..." She leaned in. "The less you eat, the longer you live. Old Chinese proverb I learned from Jinjing."

"It was too bad about her passing." Amber sighed. She missed seeing the woman around town.

"Glad you never took up smoking. It's terrible for you."

"And it makes you smell like an ash tray."

"No man in his right mind would want to kiss you," Rose added.

"Nope."

"So, what's going on with you and my grandson?" Rose sat on a stool near the sink.

"What do you mean?" Amber asked cautiously.

"I've seen you two looking goo-goo while eyeing

each other. What's your bear think? Is Shane your mate?"

"We're just friends."

Her bear rolled her eyes. Fortunately, Grandma Rose couldn't see it.

"That's what he said."

Surprise and disappointment shot through Amber.

"Don't look so sad. He was lyin' like a rug. You two are so cute, and you'd make the best babies. Why don't you *hook up* or whatever it is kids do these days?" Rose tilted her head and studied her.

"I'm not looking for a relationship right now," she said truthfully.

"How long have you been divorced now?"

"Five years. Joey was two when we signed the paperwork."

"Pft! That's long enough to grieve a good man. For a man like your ex, I'd give him six months, tops. He doesn't deserve another thought from you. Lousy no-good father," she growled.

"I'm too busy for a relationship," Amber said, taking a different approach.

"And Shane never stops working. I get it. But you have to take some time off, don't you?"

"I can't." Amber hung her head. "I'm barely

breaking even, if you count my living expenses. I need to save more money for Joey. I can't bake any more than I already do. And I still need to hire someone."

Rose shook her head, which only made Amber feel worse, as if she were a complete failure as a mother. She knew it wasn't Rose's intention by any means, but it didn't make Amber feel any better.

"You're in the prime of your life. You deserve a good mate," Rose said with conviction. "Shane's as great a man as you'll ever find. Don't wait around for him to make a move. You wait for a man, you wait forever."

"Another ancient Chinese proverb?" Amber asked.

"Ha! See, I knew you were a firecracker. He needs a woman like you in his life."

"Who needs a woman like her?" Amber's mother asked from the doorway where she lurked.

"Oh, crap," Amber muttered.

"Shane," Rose said.

"I've been telling her to marry him," Amber's mom said. "She wouldn't know a good thing if it slapped her across the face."

Rose raised a thin brow but didn't comment.

"Where's Joey?" Amber asked, changing the subject.

"He's in the dining room with Jace and Holly," her mom said.

"They're here?" All the gloom lifted in an instant. "I've got to go say hi."

Leaving Rose and her mother alone together was dangerous. Still, she told herself, they could plot all they wanted, but it wouldn't change her relationship with Shane. Even he didn't want anything more than friendship. He'd told his grandmother exactly that, so now Amber knew the truth. She couldn't deny feeling a bit of sadness, but it wasn't meant to be. Friendship would have to be enough. Besides, she'd been telling the truth when she said she wasn't ready for another relationship. She didn't know if, or when, she'd ever be able to trust another man with her heart.

4

Amber's smile grew as she walked up to Holly and Jace's table. Joey sat next to Holly while Jace sat across from them. His wheelchair leaned against the wall out of the aisle. When he spotted her, he grinned. She'd never seen him look so happy. And Holly positively glowed.

"I heard you two snuck in when I wasn't looking," Amber said.

"Guilty as charged," Jace said. "Holly was craving a milkshake, so we had to stop in. She's been dragging me around Christmas shopping all day."

"You love it," Holly said.

"Only because I'm with you." He leaned across the table and gave her a quick kiss.

"Santa Claus is behind on his shopping too."

Amber gave a slight nod toward Joey. "But Shane sent over a little helper."

"Oh really? Who?" Holly asked, craning her neck to look toward the front counter.

"Grandma Rose."

"Boy, are you in for it," Holly said wryly. "She will talk your ear off while baking up a storm. I helped her with the Christmas party cookies last year. She wore me out."

"I'm glad she's here. I could use the help. I think I bit off more than I can chew this year. Took a few too many orders."

"If you need help, we're always happy to throw on an apron," Jace said.

"Thank you for offering, but between Rose and I, there isn't a lot of extra room in the kitchen. Besides, today's orders aren't too bad. I think we can manage."

"Who's keeping an eye on Joey?" Holly asked.

"My mother was babysitting this morning. Rose offered to help this afternoon."

"How is she going to bake cookies and watch Joey?" Jace asked. "He's got a ton of energy. Even I would have trouble keeping up with him. Right, bud?"

"Can we go sledding?" Joey asked.

"Maybe later. Depends on what your mom wants

to do," Jace said. "We'd be happy to watch him so you and Rose can finish the cookies."

"Are you sure?" She hated imposing, but she really needed the help. Letting Joey run around the bakery was a recipe for disaster.

"We can take him shopping," Holly said with a twinkle in her eye.

"You told me we were done with the list." Jace crossed his arms over his chest.

"Sure. We're done with the list, but there are so many sales this year. We might find something we need that isn't on the list," Holly said.

"If it's not on the list, then we don't need it," Jace countered.

"You sound like an old, married couple already," Amber teased.

"I guess we do." Jace grinned. "Maybe I should take Joey sledding, and you can finish shopping."

"It might be nice to have you out of my hair for a few hours." Holly chuckled before leaned toward Amber. "What do men know about shopping anyway? How can you pass up a good sale?"

"Isn't that the truth?" Amber laughed.

"What time should I have him back by?" Jace asked.

"We close at five, and I should have the last batch

of cookies packed by then. Is that too long?" Amber asked.

"No, it's perfect. But before we go, we'd better get Holly that milkshake."

"I've been having the worst craving for strawberry," Holly grumbled.

"Cravings, hum?" Amber tried to discretely glance at her belly.

"I'm not pregnant. At least, I don't think I am." Holly frowned. "When was the last time..." Her eyes widened. "Um, maybe I need to stop by the drugstore later."

"Are you sick?" Joey asked, scooting away.

"No," Jace said slowly while regarding his fiancé. "She's not sick. But she might have a bun in the oven."

"What kind of bun? I like the ones with sesame seeds," Joey said.

The adults laughed.

"What?" Joey asked, perplexed.

"I'll grab your milkshake, Holly. Jace, you want anything?" Amber asked.

"I'll take one too, but chocolate. Did Joey eat lunch already?" Jace asked.

"Grandma took me to the country club."

Holly visibly stiffened before relaxing. As far as Amber knew, Holly still hadn't made up with Jace's mother, who was currently running the country club ski resort into the ground. Amber couldn't blame her for not wanting to make peace. Her mother-in-law was a real bitch.

"Can I have a milkshake?" Joey asked.

"Not today. You just had one last night. I'll bring some juice and a snack," Amber said. "Back in a minute."

When she walked into the kitchen, Rose and her mother quickly stepped away from each other. They tried to look innocent, but Amber didn't believe it for a second. They were up to something.

"How are things out in the dining area?" Rose asked. "Need me to bus dishes?"

"I can't believe you have her working for you," her mother scolded.

"I wanted to help. She shouldn't be trying to do this all alone," Rose countered with a hint of accusation in her tone.

"Well, I'd help, but I have a salon appointment in an hour." Her mother gave her daughter a pained smile. "So sorry, dear."

She wasn't sorry in the least. Amber had to force herself not to roll her eyes.

"Have fun," Amber said with more than a little sarcasm.

After her mother left, she headed over to the freezer to get ice cream for the shakes.

"She could have canceled and offered to help," Rose said as she grabbed a new mixing bowl. She began filling it with the necessary ingredients for sugar cookies.

"God forbid she break a nail," Amber muttered.

Rose laughed until she finally slapped the counter. She shook her head ruefully as she placed the bowl on the mixing stand.

After making the milkshakes, Amber took them back to Holly and Jace's table. She returned a minute later with a peanut butter and celery snack for her son.

"Be good and listen to Jace, okay?" Amber said.

"Okay, Mom." Joey grinned at Jace, who smiled back.

A twinge of guilt ate at her heart. Joey deserved a father. A good father. Not one like his deadbeat dad. Sure, he mailed his child support payments on time, but he hardly called, and he certainly hadn't come to visit since he'd left. Joey always looked so uncomfortable when he was on the phone with Fred. She hated putting him through that, but she wasn't about to stop her ex from talking to Joey. It was the least the jerk could do.

The bell on the front door rang. She looked up as Raven walked in. The woman had her head down, and her gaze darted around the bakery before landing on Amber. Raven gave her a weak smile.

"You're back," Amber said.

"Yeah. Any news on the job?" She stuffed her hands into oversized pants she'd cinched with a peeling leather belt.

"I tried calling your references but couldn't get through to anyone."

"A lot of them shut down." Raven shrugged.

She followed Amber to the front counter. When she stopped, she positioned herself so she could see the door as well as the rest of the bakery. Amber found it odd but didn't comment on it. If anything, the woman seemed scared.

"Most of your past employment was in offices. Have you ever done any baking?"

"A little. But I learn really fast. And..." Her eyes clouded. "I really need a job."

Amber studied her. There was something desperate in her eyes. She didn't seem as if she were being dishonest, but still, could Amber trust her with the keys to the store? Maybe she could hire her and then watch her for a few days before giving her access to the place.

"Here's what we'll do. I can hire you on a trial basis until Christmas. We'll see how things go and then take it from there. How does that sound?"

"It's... It sounds amazing. Thank you so much." Raven hugged her hard enough to crush her ribs. Amber gasped. "Sorry, so sorry. I'm just so grateful that you're taking a chance on me. I won't let you down, I swear. How can I help? Can I get started today? Or do you want me to wait until tomorrow?"

"If you want to work for a few hours today, I could use help with the dishes."

"I'll have them sparkling clean in no time." Raven smiled, really smiled, for the first time since Amber met her. Maybe she wasn't as gloomy as she seemed. Maybe she'd just been anxious about getting a job.

The door opened, and Shannon Wells walked in. She stomped her boots on the mat before pulling off her jacket, gloves, and hat.

"Morning!" Shannon called.

"Morning! I'll be with you in a minute. Grab a seat wherever you want," Amber said. She turned back to Raven. "Did you ever find a place to stay?"

"Not yet. But I'm working on it," she quickly added.

"I'm looking for a roommate," Shannon said.

"Really?" Raven regarded her with curiosity. "How much are you charging?"

Shannon named a rate well under market value, but Amber didn't want to correct her. Whatever she wanted to charge was her business. It also seemed like Raven needed a break.

"Can I come over and check your place out?" Raven asked.

"Sure. I'll be home in a few hours," Shannon said before rattling off directions to her ranch.

"Do you live with any men?" Raven asked.

"Uh, no." Shannon cocked her head. "Why?"

"Just curious."

"I live alone, well, with a bunch of cattle and horses. And roosters. Apparently, I have a rooster now." Shannon shrugged. "The darn thing squawks but doesn't lay eggs. It's the darndest thing."

"Roosters don't lay eggs. They're male," Raven said slowly, clearly trying to keep her voice even so she wouldn't make Shannon feel like a fool.

"Hu. Go figure. I just inherited the ranch. I can barely tell a cow from a horse."

"You didn't grow up on it?" Raven asked.

"Nope. Didn't even know my father was still alive until after he died. My mom had always told me he died before I was born. She lied. But after finding out more about my dad, I can see why she did."

"Sometimes you have to," Raven said softly.

Sweet-Talking Cowbear

Amber studied her. There was a lot going on under the surface. She hoped she wasn't making a mistake by hiring her, but what choice did she have right now? She needed to get all the Christmas orders filled.

"I'll be right out to take your order, Shannon. I've got to get Raven set up in the kitchen. I just hired her."

"You must be new in town," Shannon said.

"Just came in the other day. Seemed like a nice, quiet town," Raven said.

"Sometimes too quiet. I miss the city sometimes, but you can't beat the stars at night. The sky is gorgeous, and it goes on forever. And the people here couldn't be any nicer." Shannon smiled. "I do love Huckleberry Valley. It's such a special place."

"I felt that way when I drove through here. I was going to keep driving to Helena, but I decided to stop here," Raven said.

"Where are you from?" Amber asked.

"Oh, um. Utah."

"Salt Lake City?" Shannon asked.

"Uh, yeah." Raven's hair fell over her face, partially hiding it. "I should get to work."

Amber took her into the kitchen and introduced her to Rose, who soon had Raven working. As Amber continued her day, she kept an eye on Raven. The woman seemed quiet and more than a little shy, but she worked hard and never complained. By closing time, all the orders were filled, and the kitchen was spotless. For the first time in in weeks, Amber wasn't completely exhausted at the end of the day.

"Thank you for all your hard work," Amber told Rose and Raven.

"Ppft." Rose scoffed. "Piece of cake."

"It was fun," Raven said.

"I've got to get going. It's Bingo night," Rose said. "If you need anything, you call me. You hear?"

"Yes, Rose." Amber kissed her cheek. "Tell Shane I said hi."

"I'm sure you'll be seeing him before I do. You'll be at the Christmas party, right?" Rose asked.

"Absolutely. Shane and I are going together. As friends," she added. She didn't need Rose jumping all over that and making it into something it wasn't.

"Friends. Hum." Rose smiled. "See you Saturday."

"Thanks again for your help. I would have been frantic without you."

"Anytime, sweetie. And I'm always free to babysit Joey if you need a hand."

"You're the best."

After Rose left, Raven pulled off her apron. "Thanks for giving me a chance. Is it okay if I come back tomorrow?"

"You'd better. You work here now." Amber grinned.

"Thank you so much. It's been a while since... well, anyway. See you tomorrow."

"Five a.m. We have a lot of orders going out," Amber said.

"Five on the dot. I'll be here."

As she followed Raven out to lock the front door, Jace returned with Joey. Jace was using his wheelchair, so Joey held the door open for him.

"We went sledding and we even saw a bear and I got to ride him!" Joey shrieked as he pulled the door closed.

"A bear?" Amber raised a brow.

From behind Joey, Jace mouthed, "Wyatt."

Amber grinned. Wyatt was another one of their friends. He must have been in bear form, but Joey didn't know about it. She hadn't talked to him about shifters yet. There was plenty of time before he would experience his first shift. It was something his father should talk to him about but trying to get Fred to do anything required more effort than it was worth. Maybe Shane could talk to him when the time came.

"Thanks so much for taking him today."

"Anytime. I've got plenty of hours to fill between physical therapy appointments. And watching him gives me an excuse to procrastinate on my book even more." Jace grinned.

"You're writing a book?"

"About my time in Afghanistan. I learned quite a few lessons there about life. And it's cathartic talking about what happened."

"It sure is. I write in journals for that exact reason. I've kept them throughout the year to see how much I've grown. Although I should probably burn the ones from around the time things—" She glanced at Joey who was running around the store but still within earshot. "—ended."

"I can't imagine what that must have been like. Did you get counseling after?" Jace asked.

"No. Didn't have the money to. I just got self-help books from the library and figured out a way to move on. I had no choice, really. I had to keep things together for him." She turned her gaze to her son, who was still oblivious to the adult's conversation.

"I'm still going to Dr. Jackson. He's helped me a lot. I don't think I'd be where I'm at without him. I had to learn how to deal with my past so I could move forward. I don't think Holly and I would be engaged right now if I hadn't talked through my issues."

"I'm glad you're doing well," Amber said. "You and

Holly are perfect for each other. You're the only one who's ever been able to tame her."

"Ha!" Jace laughed. "I don't know if I'd go that far. She's still my wild woman. But I love her."

"Have you set a wedding date yet?" Amber asked.

"July 10th of next year. We debated doing it 4th of July weekend but decided against it. There are already too many events in town, and we didn't want to pull anyone away from them."

"Makes sense."

"I've got to get home, but I wasn't kidding about helping with Joey. You need anything, you call me."

"I will."

After Jace left, she grabbed her purse from the kitchen and found Joey hiding under one of the tables.

"Ready to go, little man?" she asked.

"Yep. When can I play with Jace again?"

"Maybe next week. We'll see what my schedule is like."

As they walked out into the crisp, mountain air, guilt pulled at her belly. She hated not being able to be with her son all the time. She'd never wanted to be a stay-at-home mother full time, but she felt like she spent less time with him than he needed. It was just one more way she was failing as a mother.

She sighed as she helped Joey into the passenger

seat. She helped him buckle his seatbelt before getting in to drive them home.

Later that night, after a dinner of reheated lasagna, she tucked Joey into bed.

"Can you read the one about the dinosaur again?" he asked.

"Sure."

She read to him until he fell asleep. She sat by his bed for a long time just watching him sleep. Her heart ached. She loved him more than anyone in the world, and she wanted to make sure he had a good life, which meant working all the time. It was the ultimate catch-22.

After getting ready for bed, she slid between her sheets. She pulled out her journal and wrote about her guilt for the thousandth time. No amount of writing took it away entirely, but at least she was able to lessen the pressure in her chest. Maybe one day she'd be able to spend more time with him. She just hoped it wasn't too late. At least she had friends like Jace to help her, and Shane was always willing to give her a hand.

Her entire body warmed as she pictured Shane in his paramedic outfit. It wasn't designed to be sexy at all, but she couldn't get enough of seeing him all dressed up and ready to take on any emergency. He was so damn hot. She tried not to think about him all naked and ripped underneath his clothes, but what woman in her right mind wouldn't? It was remarkable that he was still single. She'd known him for several years now. As far as she knew, he'd never dated anyone, at least not recently. So why not?

The question plagued her far into the night. One day she'd have the guts to ask him about his past relationships. Until then, she was in the dark about a huge part of his life. She wanted to get to know him even more, but wasn't that a slippery slope? What if she started thinking about him as someone other than just a friend? She'd been trying to resist seeing him as anything other than her best friend, but maybe that had been a mistake. Maybe she should take a chance and see if he was even interested. If he wasn't, then at least she'd know for sure. And if he was... well, that would be one hell of a pleasant surprise.

5
———

Shane could hardly wait to get to Amber's house to pick her and Joey up for the Huckleberry Valley Christmas Party. The huge event was the highlight of the holiday season. People came from all over Montana to share in the magical world the townspeople created in their central park. Last night, he'd helped string twinkling white lights from tree to tree, all throughout the winter wonderland. He'd stayed until the last decoration had been hung.

When he reached Amber's house, it was late afternoon. He left his truck idling so it wouldn't get cold. He walked up the front porch steps to the small, cabin-style home. Before he could knock, the door flew open and Joey came spilling out. He grabbed Shane's hand.

"I can't wait to see Santa!"

"And I'm sure he can't wait to hear what's on your list this year," Shane said. "Go hop in the truck, and we'll be right there."

"Okay!" Joey rushed out the front door.

He looked up as Amber stepped into view. His breath caught as his gaze caressed her curvy body. She wore a deep red, fitted sweater dress and a pair of thigh-high black boots. Her long, red hair curled around her face before spilling down her back in gentle waves. He tried to think of another time he'd seen her with her hair down, but he couldn't come up with anything. She was beyond gorgeous, stunning him into silence.

"Hey, stranger," she said in a sultry tone.

"You look… amazing," he said, grappling for the right word.

"Thank you. I haven't dressed up in a while, but I figured, why not get into the holiday spirit?" Her dazzling smile sent a shockwave through his belly, as if he were on a rollercoaster. "Looks like you had the same idea. That sweater is hilarious."

"When I saw it at the general store, I knew I had to have it. When else can I wear a sweater with a dinosaur Santa riding an asteroid with a Christmas tree and presents flying off the back?" He grinned.

"You should enter the ugly sweater contest."

"I don't know." He shoved his hands in his pockets so he wouldn't reach for her. "It might not be fair to the other contestants. Who could possibly win against this?" He puffed his chest.

"My favorite part is the tinsel hanging off of it." She brushed her fingertips across his sweater, coming dangerously close to his nipples.

His bear snapped awake, staring at her with a mixture of awe and desire. If Shane didn't get in the car soon, he'd have one hell of a time keeping his bear under wraps.

"We should get going." Shane's voice came out strangled and rough. He cleared his throat. "Don't want them to run out of those killer nachos before we get there, do we?"

"Definitely not. Although, I'm not sure where I'd fit them in this dress." She smoothed her hands over her hips.

He turned his back and groaned as he hurried toward his truck. On the verge of losing control, he got behind the wheel and gripped it hard. When she slid into the passenger seat, the dress rode up to reveal most of her thighs. He managed to tear his gaze away.

"There's a shuttle from the church's parking lot," she said. "That will be better than fighting for parking."

"Right." He checked the rear-view mirror to make sure Joey had his seatbelt secured.

On the way to the church, he struggled with unholy thoughts of what he'd love to do if they were alone right now. He'd never allowed himself to think of her like this before, but he couldn't help it. She was easily the most beautiful woman he'd ever known, both inside and out. She was sweet and caring and damn, those legs.

She dug through her purse and pulled out a tube of lip gloss. She swiped it over her lips, leaving a cherry-colored tint behind. The scent of strawberries filled the air. Not the chemical odor of cheap lipstick, but more like the natural smell of sun ripened berries. The urge to kiss her tugged at the part of him he struggled to control.

Suddenly, being just friends sounded idiotic. He'd been kidding himself all these years, pretending he didn't want her. He didn't just want her; he needed her. All of her. Preferably in his lap, grinding on his—

"You missed the turn," Amber said.

"Oh." He glanced to his right in time to watch the church go by. "Sorry."

"Daydreaming about cotton candy?" she teased.

"Something like that." He met her quizzical gaze before making a U-turn.

As they parked and then got onto the shuttle, he battled his bear for dominance. The beast wouldn't let up, blathering on about how she was his mate. He wasn't ready for that idea. She was his best friend, and he didn't exactly have a good track record with relationships. He hadn't even been on a date in over three years. There never seemed to be enough time, and no one had caught his eye long enough for him to consider making time.

Until now.

When they reached the festival area, peals of laughter filled the frosty air. All the holiday booths were arranged around a central ice-skating rink. At one end of the rink, a stage held Christmas carolers and a live band. On the other side, Santa Claus greeted wide-eyed children. Holiday flags flapped in the afternoon breeze, while oversized ornaments clanged together on the thirty-foot Christmas tree.

This year, the residents of the valley had voted on the theme of world peace. It seemed appropriate, considering everything going on. Ornate, decorative doves mingled with the usual sparkling ornaments in all shapes, sizes, and colors. Handmade ornaments created by the kids of Huckleberry Valley added some hometown flair.

The scents of buttery popcorn and sticky-sweet

cotton candy vied for his attention. He eyed the concession booths but decided to wait until Amber or Joey were hungry. He wanted to be able to eat dinner with them. He always enjoyed doing that, because it made him feel like he was part of a family again. He rarely got to see his parents since they'd moved to the city to be closer to the hospital. After his mother's miraculous recovery from lung cancer, they weren't taking any chances. His father wanted to keep her close to her doctors in case it ever came back.

"My mom always loved this festival," he said.

"How's she doing?" Amber asked.

He'd told her about his mom's illness and eventual dramatic recovery. Amber had been instrumental in helping him get through the ordeal of waiting. Not knowing if his mom would live or die almost destroyed him. He'd broken down a few times and Amber held him, never judging his fear and sadness as weakness. She'd been his rock, and he wasn't sure she even knew it.

"She's much better," he said.

"That's great."

"Usually, I go over there for Christmas dinner, but they're visiting friends this year. I thought about picking up an extra paramedic shift..."

"Oh." Her smile dropped.

"...but I'm not sure if I'll volunteer to work this year. I could skip it, depending on what else I've got going on. If you and Joey are free on Christmas, you could stop by. I'd have to clean my place up, but I'd love to have you over." He looked at her expectantly.

"That might be fun. But don't go to any trouble for us," Amber said. "If you don't end up working, you should come over to our place. No one should be alone on Christmas. And you usually swing by on Christmas morning anyway."

"I haven't missed a year since we became friends."

"That's true." Her smile returned. "Just let me know so I'll have enough brunch food ready."

"You don't have to do anything special for me."

"I like cooking for you." She blushed, averting her eyes. "Should we get some hot chocolate?"

"Sure." Shane's heart thumped against his ribs. The thread of electricity between them was stronger than ever, and yet he wasn't entirely sure what it meant.

It means she's our mate, his bear snapped.

Shane ignored the beast.

"I'm hungry. Can I please have a hotdog?" Joey asked.

"We'll get you one. But first, let's see what else they have," Amber said.

Without thinking, Shane held out his arm. Amber looped hers through it and moved closer to him. It felt so right, as if they were destined to be together like this. His heart thudded as they walked past the skating rink toward the food stands. What was happening to him? He'd been able to keep his feelings for her strictly friendly until now. Why was it changing? And should he put an end to it?

They stopped in front of a booth that sold hotdogs and hot chocolate. He waited until Amber and Joey put in their requests before ordering for himself. He pulled his wallet out to pay.

"Oh, no you don't, buddy." Amber pushed the hand holding the wallet down. "You bought dinner the other night. It's my turn now."

"The other night was much cheaper." He jerked his head toward the board with the prices. "These are faire prices."

"I just can't let you pay for us all the time." She gnawed on the edge of her lip.

"It's my pleasure. Besides, I feel less like a piggie when I pay. I did order two hotdogs for myself. And a large drink. And I'm about to go to the next booth to get either cotton candy or a caramel apple or a funnel cake or maybe all of the above." He grinned.

"How about this? You buy dinner, and I'll buy dessert. I'm sure Joey will want a bite."

"Deal."

"What's a funnel cake?" Joey asked.

"Oh, boy, are you in for a treat!" Shane smiled at Amber. In a mock-horrified tone, he asked, "What kind of mother doesn't introduce her son to ten thousand calories of pure sugar?"

"The kind that doesn't have the energy to chase after him for the rest of the night." She laughed.

"I'll keep an eye on him," Shane said.

"Want to go ice skating later?" Amber asked Joey.

"Yay!"

"That's the trick." She leaned toward Shane and whispered conspiratorially. "You can give the little monster sugar as long as you have a way to work it off afterward."

"Good to know." He bumped his shoulder against hers.

"Follow me for more kid tricks," she joked.

"I'd follow you forever," he blurted.

She stood so close her breath caressed his cheeks. Hers went rosy as she stared at him. A questioning desire shimmered in her eyes. He couldn't look away. He moved incrementally closer, never taking his eyes off hers. Her plump, pink lips glistened in the setting sunlight. Lights twinkling overhead cast a halo around her hair. He was just a breath away when someone yelled his name.

"Shane! Order up for four hotdogs and three hot chocolates!" the concession woman hollered, breaking the spell.

"I'll go get it," he told Amber.

"Um, I'll find a seat over there." She pointed toward a collection of picnic tables covered in festive tablecloths.

As he went to grab the food, he let out a shaky breath. He'd never wanted to kiss anyone so much before. Never. He hadn't kissed a woman in years, but he wanted to end that drought with her. Not just because she was a beautiful woman, but because she was special. Different. The most amazing woman he'd ever known, really. So why was it so hard to take that first step?

Amber found an empty table near the skating rink. Despite the chilly air, she was burning up. A drop of sweat traced a path between her breasts. She fanned her face to try to cool her cheeks. Had Shane almost kissed her? She could have sworn he was getting closer and closer until the concession lady had called his name.

Her bear growled deep in her chest. It didn't like the fact that another woman was calling his name. He didn't belong to them, but her bear didn't care. It wanted him to be their mate, and it wouldn't listen to reason.

Why can't we mate with him? her bear asked silently.

Because he's our friend.

Friends fall in love all the time.

How do you know that? Amber asked, perplexed.

Chick-flicks, duh! You make us watch all those girl movies about best friends falling in love. Her bear rolled her eyes.

Do I? She thought back to the last few movies she'd rented online. Crap! The beast was right. She'd been watching a bunch of movies like that. It was probably time for more action flicks instead.

See, her bear said smugly.

"Okay fine, no more chick-flicks," she muttered.

"What was that?" Shane asked when he arrived with the food.

"Mommy talks to herself sometimes," Joey said. He grinned as if he knew he wasn't being helpful.

"Really?" Shane sat then passed out the food, an amused smile on his face.

"I only talk to myself when I'm feeling particularly growly," she said, hoping Shane would get the hint that she was talking to her bear.

"I get growly myself too," he said. The glint in his eyes told her he understood.

While they ate, she watched the ice skaters to avoid turning her puppy dog eyes on him. Having him so close was making her want things she'd never wanted before. How would he react if she told him she was interested in more than friendship?

Testing where he stood became more and more appealing as time passed. They finished their food, and she bought a cinnamon apple funnel cake for the three of them to share. She took a huge bite, letting the powdered sugar coat her tongue. And in an instant, she wondered what *he* tasted like.

A quick inhale of breath sucked sugar into her lungs. She coughed, and a cloud of powder billowed out and across the table, hitting Shane right in the face.

"Oh my God." She choked before taking a sip of hot chocolate. It burned all the way down and did nothing to stop the spasming of her lungs.

"Are you okay?" Shane quickly moved around the

table to sit by her side. He gently patted her back. "You're supposed to eat it, not inhale it."

"I know." She managed between hacks.

Inside, her bear shook with laughter. It sat on its butt and grabbed it heels, rolling around in her chest. The little brat loved laughing at her expense.

"Mommy, can I go skate now?" Joey asked.

"Here." Shane pulled out his wallet and handed some cash to him. "Go get your skates and stay inside the rink. When you're done, skate over here and let me know. I'll come get you."

"Okay!"

Amber watched through watering eyes as Joey ran off toward the rental stand.

"I've got my eye on him," Shane said. "You okay? Can I get you some water?"

"I'm fine. Thank you."

"Good, because for a second there I thought I might have to do CPR on you." He shifted closer and his thigh brushed hers. Molten heat seeped up from where they'd touched to warm her deep inside.

She giggled nervously as his steady gaze held hers. She swallowed, unable to think of a snappy comeback.

"Your hair got caught." He cupped her cheek and used his thumb to brush the hair off what was left of her lip gloss. He didn't let her go.

"Shane," she whispered.

He wrapped his arm around her waist and pulled her closer. She leaned toward him, unable to tear her gaze away from his sensual lips.

"Would this be a terrible idea?" he asked softly.

"I... I don't know," she admitted, because it was the damn truth.

"We're such good friends," he murmured.

Is that all? She wanted to scream, but she couldn't make her mouth move.

He gently kissed her temple before sitting back. His jaw was slightly clenched, but relaxed as he took a sip of his drink. Although he wasn't looking directly at her, she sensed his alertness and awareness. Was he waiting for her to make a move? Should she? If only the path were clear.

"I'm stuffed," he said, pushing the dessert plate toward her.

"I think I'm done with sugar for today." She gave him a soft smile.

"Did you put your tree up yet?" he asked.

"I bought it, but it's been sitting in the garage for the last few days. Honestly, I tried to get it in the stand, but it kept falling over so I gave up."

"When we get back to your place, I'll set it up for you."

"You're so sweet."

"What are friends for?" He smiled.

Friends. Well, shit.

"What does your work week look like next week?" he asked.

"I've still got a bunch of orders, but I hired Raven."

"Really? Were you able to verify her employment?"

"No. But she works her butt off. I feel like I can trust her. You know how you just have that feeling sometime?"

"Yeah. But I also believe in the saying, trust but verify. I'd still try contacting her old employers. Or at least try running a background check on her. The sheriff can help with it or you can do it online. You'll just need her social security number."

"I'll do that. In the meantime, I'm not giving her the keys to the store until I'm sure I can trust her completely."

"I'm off most of next week, so if you need help baking, I can come over."

"You should enjoy a day off without feeling like you have to help me all the time." Guilt reared its ugly head once again.

"I enjoy helping you. It makes me feel… needed."

"I really don't know what I'd do without you."

His gaze turned intent for a moment before he

looked away. He pressed his lips together before flicking out his tongue to lick them. She had no idea what it meant, but he was thinking hard about something. She wanted to ask what was on his mind, but also didn't want to know. What if he was thinking about how much she took advantage of their friendship?

She cursed herself for even considering being more than friends. Sure, it seemed like he was flirting a bit, but was he? Or was it just wishful thinking on her part?

As she watched Joey skate around the rink, she couldn't shake the total body awareness she felt every time she was close to Shane. Yearning tugged at her heart, and even though she knew she couldn't act on it, the feeling wouldn't go away. It was as if she were on a runaway train destined to derail and ruin their friendship. She'd have to stop testing the waters with him and stick to strictly friendship. As much as she hated admitting it, she truly needed him to help her with Joey. Falling for Shane would only ruin her currently stable life, and the last thing she needed to do was throw her life into turmoil again.

6

Shane couldn't stop kicking himself for not kissing Amber properly. He'd seen the desire simmering in her eyes, but the warning signals coming from his heart stopped him. He'd never been good at relationships. He'd only really ever had one long-term girlfriend, and that was years ago. He wasn't sure he even knew how to date anymore. Neglecting that part of his life put him at a strict disadvantage. He was way out of practice, and Amber wasn't someone he wanted to practice on. She deserved better.

He picked at the last few bites of funnel cake. Fidgeting around on the bench, he couldn't keep his energy in check. All of the frustration built and built until he had to do something to release it.

"Want to go skating with me?" he asked.

"That sounds fun, but I'm wearing a dress."

"There are other women out there in dresses too. Some are even shorter." *Hello, mouth? Meet my foot.* He cringed, even though she didn't seem to notice his faux pas.

"As long as I don't fall, it should be fine. And I do have leggings on," she mused.

"Great! Let's go." He stood and helped her out of the bench.

When they reached the rental area, a pimply-faced kid asked their sizes and handed them ice skates.

"I don't think I've been skating in years," she said.

"Who taught Joey how to?"

"My mother." Her mouth turned down. "Just one more thing she holds over my head."

"I'm surprised she wanted to do something that might mess up her hair." He smirked.

"Seriously." Amber laughed. "I think she had the hots for an Olympic skating instructor who was staying at the country club for a few weeks last year. Suddenly, she wanted to take Joey to skate every other day. It worked out well for me, but she always has an ulterior motive."

As she stepped onto the ice, her skate slid out from under her. Shane grabbed her before she could fall.

After helping her get her balance, he took her hand. They started skating and merged into the circle of skaters.

"It must be hard having your mom nitpicking everything you do," he said.

"It's annoying as hell. I think she means well, but it just doesn't come out right."

"The way she talks to you isn't right. She should be offering support, not condemning you for being a bad mother. Which you're not," he quickly added.

"Thanks for saying that. Sometimes I feel like I can't get anything right. Joey spends more time with other people than he spends with me. The bakery takes up all my time. If I ever had the money to expand, I could sell more and afford to hire a manager so I wouldn't have to be there all the time."

"I do that with the ranch. There's no way I could do both jobs alone."

"You'd mentioned that you were thinking about cutting back on hours." She increased the pace slightly.

"I keep going back and forth on it," he admitted.

"If you don't need the money, why work so hard?"

"It's... I just want to be useful."

"Working on the ranch is useful. The animals would probably be happy to have you around more."

Sweet-Talking Cowbear

"Only because I bribe them with treats." Her laughter warmed his soul.

"I try to avoid that with Joey, but sometimes I feel like I'm buying his love, one milkshake at a time." She shook her head slightly.

"He loves you, milkshakes or not." He squeezed her hand. "I think you're being way too hard on yourself."

"Maybe." She went silent for several minutes before saying, "Did I ever tell you that I took figure skating lessons?"

"No! Let me see a spin or something." He released her hand and skated closer to the center where people were showing off their fancier skating moves.

She grinned before digging one skate into the ice. She did a little jump before pushing off faster and faster, gaining speed then leaping into a spiraling spin. Landing on one foot, she spread her arms out. Her face tilted up as if basking in the glow of approval from a crowd. He clapped wildly before putting his fingers in his mouth and whistling. Several people turned to watch her.

Over the next few minutes, she twirled and spun and skated circles around him. His cheeks hurt from grinning non-stop. Pure joy radiated from her smile.

She needed more of this. More unbridled happiness. And he wanted to give it to her.

"Ready to do a lift?" she yelled.

"A what?" His eyes went wide as she skated straight for him. Did she want him to lift her overhead? He panicked, and every way it could possibly go wrong played through his mind in a flash. He'd drop her for sure. Not because she was curvy, but because he had no idea what he was doing.

"Go!" She jumped at the last second. He fumbled to try to grab her waist but missed. They went tumbling into a ball. Hysterical laughter blasted from her plump, pink lips. She lay on top of him, pinning him to the ice, but he wasn't cold at all. He was burning up and was afraid he might melt the whole damn rink.

"You're terrible at lifts," she teased.

"Maybe, but I'm not terrible at this."

He laced his hand through her hair and cupped the back of her head. A soft gasp escaped her mouth right before he swept his lips across hers. He deepened the kiss, figuring it might be his only opportunity to kiss her like this. Gliding his tongue across the seam of her mouth, he pressed slightly. Her lips parted, giving him a chance to taste her. She was all hot chocolate and powdered sugar, and uniquely sweet.

Her tongue melted against his, and a shiver rippled through her body into his.

Taking full advantage of the situation, he explored her mouth with his tongue, not daring to open his eyes. She wasn't pulling away. In fact, she was pressing even closer. One of her thighs slid across his, and soon she was straddling him.

"Get a room!" someone yelled.

She jerked back and was on her feet in an instant. Dazed, he slowly rolled onto his hands and knees before standing. Before he could say anything, she skated off into the throng of people. He had to race to catch up to her.

When he reached her side, he glanced at her expression out of the corner of his eye. She didn't look angry. If anything, she looked mortified. The whole kiss couldn't have lasted more than a few seconds, but everyone in town had to have seen it. And if they hadn't, word would spread like wildfire. The gossips of Huckleberry Valley salivated over any new relationships. By morning, everyone would know he'd kissed her. But it didn't bother him one bit. Would it bother her?

When she headed for the exit to the rink, he followed. She stepped onto the wooden path and walked back to the rental area. They sat side by side on a bench to remove their skates. She still hadn't looked at him or said anything. Her cheeks were bright pink, but he wasn't sure if it was due to the cold, or if it was due to embarrassment.

After they turned in their skates, she pulled her thigh-high boots on. He quickly slipped into his cowboy boots before looking at her. She turned to him and started laughing.

"What's so funny?" he asked.

"Everyone's going to think we've been secretly having an affair."

"You have to be married to have an affair, right?" He tilted his head, confused by her response to the kiss.

"I don't know." She chuckled. "At least Fred never cheated on me. Maybe with his job, but that's not really cheating, is it?"

It was a rhetorical question he didn't bother answering.

"I should go get Joey. It's getting late." She stood.

"Amber." He grabbed her hand and led her out of earshot of other people, while maintaining an eye on Joey, who was still skating.

"Hum?" She swallowed, dropping her gaze.

"I hope I didn't cross any lines just now."

"We just got caught up in the moment. That's all." She still wouldn't look at him.

"Right."

"We'll meet you at the shuttle stop in a few minutes," she said as she walked away.

As he watched her walk toward the rink and call for Joey, he sighed. He didn't regret the kiss one bit but doing it in a public place had been a terrible idea. Now she'd have to field questions about them all day. He'd put her into a bad position, and now she probably regretted kissing him back. But she *did* kiss him back.

He hooked his thumbs in the belt loops on his jeans. As he headed toward the shuttle stop, several people nodded in his direction before whispering to whomever was standing beside them. He wanted to say something, but what? He couldn't deny kissing her. Hell, he didn't want to deny it either. Kissing her had been a thousand times better than any of his fantasies. But she didn't seem to feel the same way. Was it because he'd kissed her in front of everyone, or because she really wasn't interested?

Maybe their friendship was the problem. He didn't want to do anything to ruin it, but he already wanted to kiss her again. And again. All night long, if she'd let him.

Damn, he was in a world of trouble now.

. . .

AMBER'S FACE burned as she waited for Joey to exchange his skates for his boots. She couldn't raise her eyes without meeting someone's questioning glance. Her lips still tingled from where he'd kissed her. And damned if she didn't want him again.

"Mommy?" Joey asked as he stood.

"Yeah, hon?"

"Why were you and Shane kissing?"

Oh, boy.

"We, um, fell down and..." She struggled for the right words. She didn't want to lie about it to her son, but how could she explain it in a way he'd understand?

"I like him. He's my friend," Joey said.

"My friend too."

"I don't kiss my friends. That would be gross!" Joey's little face screwed up.

Amber chuckled and grasped her son's hand. As she walked toward the shuttle stop, she ran through a bunch of different explanations for why she kissed Shane. Nothing seemed appropriate to tell him. She wasn't even sure she had to justify the kiss, but she also didn't want Joey to think there was anything going on between her and Shane.

When they reached the meeting point, Joey released her hand and ran to wrap his arms around Shane's leg.

"What's up, buddy?" Shane asked, perplexed.

"Are you going to be my new daddy?"

Amber froze.

Shane froze.

Their gazes met. Shane raised a brow as if to ask her what he should say. She had no idea how to respond. Panic welled up inside her. Joey needed stability and security. Having a fling with Shane was out of the question. Not that he'd asked.

The shuttle bus arrived. It saved her from having to explain the unexplainable. As they got onto the bus, Joey slid into one long seat. Amber sat next to him, while Shane took the aisle spot.

Sitting between Shane and Joey, Amber couldn't focus. Her heart and her mind warred for how to deal with what had just happened. She wanted him. She definitely wouldn't deny it if he ever asked, but was that enough for a relationship? She'd wanted her ex too and look how that turned out.

They were silent for the ride back to the parking lot. On the way home, Joey chattered on about all the fun he'd had at the festival. He talked about the friends he'd seen and what everyone had eaten for dinner.

Amber tried to listen, but she couldn't focus, especially not with Shane's rock-hard thigh pressed against hers. He wasn't doing it on purpose. The bench was only really designed for two people. Still, the contact sent tendrils of desire from her belly to her wet center. The sensation didn't abate, even after they got into Shane's truck to drive home. They weren't touching anymore, but she could still feel him under her. The way he'd arched slightly against her when she'd straddled him flickered in her memory. Her nipples tightened, and she squirmed in the seat.

"Did you still want me to set up your tree?" Shane asked softly.

"Um..." She glanced into the rear-view mirror at Joey. He grinned. "Sure."

"It will only take a few minutes, and then I'll be out of your hair."

"You don't have to rush," she said.

"Okay. I wasn't sure..."

"It's okay. Things happen and... even if they were nice things, it's not always the right time for them," she said.

"Nice?" He gave her a sidelong look.

"Okay, better than nice." She smoothed her hands over her thighs.

"After we tuck him in, we should talk about it."

"We don't have to," she said, offering him an out.

"I want to. I'm not a fan of tension."

"I'm not tense," she said, tensing.

"Good." He gave her an amused smile.

A few minutes later, they reached her house. She opened the door and stepped into the cold, dark interior.

"Darn it, I forgot to set the heater," she said.

"Want me to start a fire?" Shane asked, nodding toward the fireplace.

"Sure. Thank you. I'll turn on the heater anyway. I'm trying to cut back on wood use because of the smoke. It's not good for your lungs, and I want Joey to grow up big and strong. I don't want him to get asthma like Fred."

"I didn't know you could get it from wood smoke."

"Well, I'm not totally sure, but I'm not taking any chances. I'm trying to do whatever it takes to protect him."

"You're a good mom," Shane said.

The gentleness in his eyes made hers well with tears. After turning away to adjust the thermostat, she blinked rapidly. She didn't go back to where Shane stood until she was sure she wouldn't burst out crying. He was the only person in the world who ever told her she was doing a good job as a parent. She needed that reassurance more than he could ever know.

"The tree's out in the garage," she said.

"I'll get it."

"The door's through the kitchen."

As he headed toward the door, she glanced at his butt more than once. She wanted to feel him under her again. She wanted to be in his strong, sexy arms. Yearning tugged at her soul. It wasn't just his body; it was everything about him. She just wanted to be closer to him in every way.

"Got it," Shane called as he carried the tree through the door.

"Let me grab the stand." She went into the garage and fetched it.

When they returned to the living room, they found Joey lying on the couch. His sleepy eyes opened.

"Someone needs to go to sleep," she said, setting the stand down in the corner of the room between the window and the fireplace. Shane chuckled as he leaned the tree against the wall before squatting to fiddle with the stand.

"But I want to put ornaments on," Joey protested.

"We can trim the tree tomorrow," she said.

"Can Shane come over and help?"

"I don't know." She turned to Shane and grinned. "Can he?"

"Well, I was going to hang out with my cows all

day, but..." He left a dramatic pause. "I *guess* I could come help you. But only if there's tinsel."

"Yay! Tinsel!" Joey's eyes sparkled with joy.

"Oh, no. Remember what happened to grandma's cat last year?" she asked.

"It pooped it out." Joey giggled before turning serious. "I had to pull it out of his butt!"

"I didn't make him do that," she said. "I heard the cat screeching and came out to find a mess."

"Gross," Shane said.

"So, no tinsel in this house ever again," she said.

"Or just don't let your mom bring the cat," Shane suggested.

"Good luck with that." Amber snorted. "Come on, Joey. It's off to bed. Say goodnight to Shane."

"Night, Shane," Joey mumbled as his eyelids drooped.

"Night, buddy."

Amber almost asked Shane if he wanted to help tuck Joey in but decided against it. That would be far too domestic, and it would send the wrong message. She wasn't even sure what message she was trying to send, if any. She still wasn't sure what to do about her attraction to Shane.

There, she'd admitted it to herself. She was lusting after the guy. But lust wasn't a good enough excuse to pursue a relationship. She'd found that out the hard way.

For now, she'd have to take things one day at a time. At least she could stop lying to herself about how much she wanted him. It was a small step forward. It was better than standing still. But she wasn't quite ready to run into his arms yet. She'd have to feel things out and see if Shane just wanted her for sex, or something more.

7

Amber took one last look at her sleeping son before closing his bedroom door. She walked back into the living room to find Shane tangled in Christmas tree lights. She stifled a giggle. He'd secured the tree in the stand and had added water to keep it fresh. A fire crackled in the fireplace, and two empty wine glasses sat on the coffee table. She eyed them quizzically.

"A little help here." He gave her a sheepish grin.

"Didn't know you were into bondage," she teased.

"I'm a man of many secrets." He waggled his eyebrows.

"And here I was thinking you were vanilla to the core." She picked through the strands, trying to find one of the ends. "Wow, you've got this really twisted up."

"In my defense, they were in a ball in the box I found. I went back into the garage because I saw the box labeled lights and ornaments. I hope you don't mind. I wanted to get it all set up so you wouldn't have to tomorrow."

"It's okay." She laughed as she finally found an end.

She circled him, slowly unwinding the strings of lights. Several times, she had to slip her hand between the lights and his body. She could have sworn she felt him tremble at least once.

Being this close was unnerving. His woodsy scent reminded her of a snow-covered clearing in a pine forest. Steady, peaceful, and grounded. Like Shane.

"There," she said, breathlessly.

"You're really good at unraveling things," he said softly.

There was a hint of something in his voice that sent butterflies fluttering through her belly. The intensity of his gaze warmed her from the outside in, until she was smoldering for him. Suddenly, her sweater dress was too warm. The wild side of her she hadn't acknowledged since becoming a mother reared. The impulse to pull off her dress and throw him on the couch came out of nowhere to claw at her control. She willed her feet to move so she could back away, but they wouldn't cooperate.

Hypnotized by the shadow of desire in his eyes, her mouth went dry. She wet her lips with a quick flick of her tongue. His gaze dropped to her mouth. A low groan escaped his lips as he slowly closed the distance between them.

She gazed at him through lowered lashes. Even though she knew what was coming, her heart still kicked when his lips met hers. The kiss started out gentle and sweet but morphed into something hot and passionate. She couldn't come up with a single good reason to hold back. She succumbed to his strength, to his touch, to his possessive grip when he circled his arms around her and crushed her against his chest.

His tongue, hot and insistent, pushed past her lips. She groaned and slid her hands up from his back to wrap them around his neck. His cowboy hat fell off, landing on the floor, forgotten as he backed her toward the couch.

In one fluid motion, she was on her back. He covered her, pressing her into the pillows, kissing her until she thought she might float away on a cloud of pure pleasure.

When his hand slid up the outside of her thigh,

she parted her legs. He was still fully clothed, but the evidence of his arousal pressed against her core. Her dress was up around her waist. His hands slipped up to cup her breasts. Deft fingers moved her silky bra out of the way. She gasped as the warmth of his hands covered her aching nipples.

He tore his mouth away from hers to kiss the edge of her jaw. She'd never been so swept away. She clutched his shoulders, holding on as he pulled the dress higher to reveal her breasts. Things were going fast. Too fast. She couldn't keep up with the sensations rioting through her body.

"Shane," she whispered.

"Mm..." He nibbled her earlobe.

"I..." She trailed off, unable to verbalize the warring feelings inside.

He must have sensed her hesitation, because he backed off immediately. He sat back on his heels and smoothed her dress down.

"I'm sorry. I shouldn't have—"

"No, it's—"

"I don't know what I'm doing." He shook his head slightly. "I wasn't here for this. I didn't mean to take advantage of anything."

"You didn't." She sat and adjusted her dress. "I got carried away too."

"If you weren't my best friend," he murmured.

"That's been my issue too."

"I don't want to screw up what we have," he said softly, caressing the back of her hand with the tips of his fingers.

"Me neither. Which is why... God, this is so stupid." She shook her head. "I want you, Shane. It wasn't always like this, but recently, I don't know. Something... changed."

He sighed and leaned his forehead to touch hers. He pulled her into a gentle embrace. "If I knew for sure this could be something..."

"You wouldn't be so hesitant?" she offered.

"Exactly."

"I know what you mean." She let him pull her sideways into his lap. She twisted to look at him. His mouth was so close, so sweet and sensual.

"Don't look at me like that," he murmured, stroking her back. "I'm still a man, not a monk."

"I know." She wriggled in his lap, and he groaned.

"So, what are we going to do about this?" he asked.

She wasn't sure, so she kissed him instead. His arms went around her once more, pulling her close. She took control of the kiss, sliding her tongue against his, pulling back to soften her lips before delving in once more. His hands dropped to her hips. He held her tightly while pressing up against her. When she finally broke away, they were both panting.

She wanted to take him to bed, but she also didn't want to rush into anything she might regret later. She couldn't believe she was in his lap, kissing him. Shane. Her best friend. What the heck was she thinking?

He held her close, stroking her back, not saying anything, just being with her, the way he always was. She snuggled closer and rested her head on his shoulder. He brushed his lips across her cheek.

Across the room, his phone buzzed and jingled a shrill ring.

"Ugh! I have to get that. It's dispatch." He lifted her out of his lap and onto the couch. He answered the phone. "Colt… Um, hum. Downtown? Which buildings? Okay. I'll meet the team there."

"What's going on?" Amber asked.

"There's a fire downtown. I don't know which buildings are affected. I've got to go." He gave her a quick kiss before cupping her cheeks. "I'll talk to you tomorrow. This isn't over."

She turned her head to kiss his palm. A soft intake of breath swelled his chest. He smiled before heading toward the door.

As he walked out, she wrapped her arms across her body. She walked to the window and watched him drive off into the snowy night. She wasn't sure if finally kissing him would be the start of anything, but she hoped it would. She'd spent too many years alone and being with him just felt right. Hopefully, the spark they'd started tonight would burn into something more.

Shane's heart plunged as he drove down Main Street. Angry flames licked the sky. Black smoke billowed up, infusing the night air with the acrid scent of burning plastic. An orange glow guided him down the street, past business after business. The scream of nearby sirens sent his nerves on edge.

"Please don't let it be the bakery," he prayed harder than he'd ever prayed in his life.

His bear jumped to attention, alerted by his fear. It paced across his chest, waiting for any sign that it might need to burst free. He pushed the beast down, telling it to stay calm. He'd never had his bear break free, but in times of high stress, the beast threatened to explode out of him.

Shane leaned forward. The streetlights were out. The whole downtown area seemed to have lost power. Flashing lights from Sheriff's Deputy trucks strobed across the buildings like something out of a horror movie. The general store was untouched. A Very Huckleberry Christmas Boutique still stood. The café's windows were dark without any hint of flames. The further he drove, the more his stomach dropped.

"Shit!"

The bakery was engulfed in flames. An apocalyptic roar filled the air. Support beams cracked and fell, casting a cloud of sparks into the sky. Glass littered the sidewalk, reflecting the blaze inside the building.

Firetrucks wailed as they reached the scene. They parked haphazardly, cutting off access to the area. Firemen jumped out and got to work, hooking up hoses before running toward the flames.

Shane slammed the brakes on his truck and squealed into a makeshift parking space, well out of the way of the firemen. He jumped out of his truck and ran toward the scene. Further down the sidewalk, another paramedic stood over a body. Buckley, Shane's coworker, was giving the victim mouth-to-mouth resuscitation and chest compressions. Sweat trickled down his brow. His face was red from exertion.

"One. Two. Three…" Buckley counted.

"Let me take over," Shane said.

Buckley moved out of the way, heaving with exhaustion.

"Found her inside. Pulled her out. Not breathing. No pulse," Buckley gasped.

Shane's heart stalled. Pale skin, black hair, blue eyes, this had to be Amber's new employee, Raven. The horrific scent of charred hair almost made him gag. He'd rescued more than a few fire victims over the years, but he still couldn't get past that smell. He quickly checked her for burns but didn't see anything obvious. Still assessing, he put two fingers over the vein in her wrist. A thin thread of life pulsed against his fingers.

"I got something," he yelled. He placed his hand over the victim's mouth. The air didn't move. "She still isn't breathing."

He tilted her head back, checking her airway before pinching her nostrils together with his thumb and forefinger. There wasn't any time to grab his protective mask. He sealed his lips over her mouth and immediately started rescue breaths. He breathed into her mouth for one second. Her chest rose. Her airway wasn't blocked. He breathed again.

"Come on."

He repeated the breaths then checked again to make sure she still had a pulse.

"How long has she been down?" Shane asked.

"Not sure," Buckley said.

Shane breathed into her mouth again. Her chest rose, but she still wasn't breathing on her own.

He repeated the breaths for what seemed like hours. Only a minute or two had passed, but CPR always twisted time into a long tendril of fear. He pushed away doubt. He wasn't going to lose her. Not on his watch.

"Let me take over," Buckley said, leaning in.

"No, I've got this." Shane elbowed Buckley back before giving her another rescue breath.

"Dammit, you're going to get tired. Let's switch over."

"One more," Shane said, knowing his partner was right. CPR could become extremely exhausting quickly, regardless of what kind of shape someone was in. Shane could run a mile in eight minutes, but he'd still struggle to keep up the correct CPR pace if he didn't take a break.

"Move!" Buckley took over, working on her until he motioned for Shane to jump back in.

At least five minutes passed, and she still didn't regained consciousness. He debated grabbing a manual resuscitator from the ambulance, but he didn't want to leave her. Buckley must have read his mind, because he ran off before returning with it.

Shane was positioning it over her when Raven

sucked in a breath. Shane's heart kicked. Raven coughed violently. A look of sheer panic filled her eyes. She tried to shove him, but he didn't budge.

"We're here to help you," Shane said. "Just take a few breaths. Does anything hurt?"

"Lungs," she gasped.

"It's probably smoke inhalation. Does anything else hurt?"

"My head." She touched the back of her head. Blood smeared across her fingertips. Her eyes widened before rolling back.

"Raven! Stay with me. I need you awake," Shane commanded.

"It hurts," she whimpered.

"We'll get you to the hospital," Shane said. Buckley handed him an oxygen mask which was connected to a portable O_2 cylinder. Shane placed the mask over her nose and mouth. "Just breathe normally."

"I... Can't!" Panicked, she tried to pull the mask away. She stared frantically over his shoulder, as if looking for someone.

"You're okay. You're safe," he reassured her.

"I'll get the stretcher," Buckley said.

"Can you tell me what happened?" Deputy Bullock demanded, towering over them.

Shane hadn't even seen the sheriff's deputy until

now. He never showed up to anything on time. And when he did, he interfered more than he helped.

"She needs to be transported right now. You can ask her questions later." Shane glared at the deputy.

Buckley arrived with a stretcher. They lifted her onto it. Buckley placed a blanket over her before wheeling her toward the waiting ambulance.

"I'll follow you guys," Deputy Bullock blustered.

Shane ignored the oaf. No one liked the guy, but they still had to deal with him. Unfortunately, the sheriff hadn't felt the need to fire him, despite the rumors and trouble Bullock caused.

After climbing into the back of the ambulance, Shane pulled the doors closed. He rapped on the front, giving Buckley the go-head to drive. With the siren running, they rushed out of town toward Bozeman. The hospital was thirty minutes away on a good day. With all the snow, it would take a bit longer.

He checked Raven's vitals. Her pulse was too fast, and her breathing was labored. The bump on the back of her head was the biggest concern. She could have a brain injury. He held her hand to try to keep her calm.

"Just take slow breaths," he said softly.

"I'm sorry," she choked.

Sorry? His back went rigid. Why was she sorry? Had she set the fire?

"What happened?" he asked. He knew he shouldn't be trying to get her to talk, but he needed to know if she caused the fire.

"He got me."

"He, who?"

She closed her eyes. A single tear ran down her soot-covered face. She shivered. He checked for signs of shock. Her skin was pale and clammy. Sweat dotted her brow. He raised her feet twelve inches then added a second blanket. He checked her vitals again. She wasn't in immediate danger, but she wasn't out of the woods either. He silently willed Buckley to drive faster.

"You're going to be all right," he said, trying to reassure her. The calmer he could keep her, the better. She didn't respond, but she breathed at a more normal rate now.

The ambulance ride felt like it was taking forever, but they'd only been driving for fifteen minutes. Alternating between checking her vitals and glancing outside to monitor their progress, he tried to stay focused. He couldn't think about the fact that Amber's bakery was burning down. He'd been to enough fires to know that the blaze would level the building. His heart ached. How on earth was he going to tell her?

He glanced at his phone but decided against calling. He had a job to do, and he couldn't afford to be distracted. He'd have to wait to talk to her.

When they arrived at the hospital, doctors and nurses met them at the ambulance loading bay. He rattled off the vitals, information about her head injury and suspicion of shock before turning the patient over to them.

"We've got it from here," a nurse said.

As they rolled her into the hospital, Shane slumped against the back of the ambulance. Adrenalin coursed through his body, making him lightheaded. His hands shook.

"You okay?" Buckley asked.

"Yeah." He clenched his hands several times to try to relax.

"I can't believe the bakery's on fire. I wonder what happened."

"I smelled gasoline," Shane said.

"At the scene?"

"Pretty sure that's what I smelled. You ever been to an arson scene?" Shane asked.

"Not recently. Back when I worked in the city, I caught one or two, but it's been years." Buckley grabbed a bottle of water from their ice chest and handed it to Shane.

Sweet-Talking Cowbear

"We'll have to see what the sheriff finds out. I hope it was an accident. Amber's going to be devastated."

"Are you going to call her?" Buckley asked.

"No. I should tell her in person. I was at her place when the call came in. We didn't know it was the bakery. Just a fire on Main."

"Let's get back. She should hear it from a friend," Buckley said.

"Yeah."

Shane got into the passenger side of the ambulance. As they drove back, his jaw clenched. He hoped he hadn't actually smelled gasoline, but deep down, he knew he had. Arson. Who would want to burn down the bakery? And why? As far as he knew, Amber didn't have any enemies. Her ex was a jerk, but he wasn't a criminal.

And what was Raven doing there in the middle of the night? Did she have something to do with it? She'd said, "He found me." He who? Was someone after her? Was that why she was so secretive about her past on her job application? Was she even who she claimed she was?

Anxiety and anger coiled tight in his chest. He had to take a few breaths to try to calm down, but it was no use. Amber had just lost everything. Well, not everything. She still had Joey and her house. And she still had Shane. No matter what happened, he was determined to be there for her. As a friend for sure, but maybe as something more.

He couldn't think about their relationship right now. He had to focus on helping her through the loss of her business. But first, he had to tell her. And he knew she wasn't going to take the news well.

8

Amber tossed and turned as sleep eluded her. Kissing Shane had sent her into a mental tailspin of possibilities. Until now, she'd done everything she could to resist her attraction to him. She'd been in denial, because facing the truth held to many risky unknowns. But now that she'd felt the sweet caress of his lips on hers, it was all she could think about.

A soft knock sounded on the window. She jumped and pulled the blankets up to her neck. According to the clock on her nightstand, it was just after three a.m. Who on earth could be at her window at this time of night?

She quietly slipped out of bed and grabbed the baseball bat she kept beside it. Although she never worried about crime in Huckleberry Valley, it was easier to sleep at night, knowing she had a way of defending herself if she needed it.

As she crept toward the window, her heart pounded. She slowly pushed back the curtain while gripping the bat tighter.

Shane's face appeared. The breath she'd been holding whooshed out of her lungs. She pushed up the window.

"What are you doing here?" she asked.

"I need to talk to you. I would have gone to the front door, but I didn't want to wake Joey."

The serious look in his eyes sent warning sirens off in her head. On the way to the front door to let him in, she knew something was really wrong. She was almost afraid to open the door, because somewhere deep inside she knew why he was there.

"Come in," she said softly.

He took his cowboy hat off and stepped inside. The acrid scent of smoke clung to his jacket, wafting into the house as he removed it. He slowly hung it on the coat rack. He avoided eye contact until they sat on her sofa together.

He turned to her and grasped both her hands in his. "I have news about the bakery."

Her mouth opened, but she couldn't push sound past the lump in her throat.

"There was a fire downtown. Several shops were involved in the blaze."

"Was anyone hurt?" she asked, delaying what she knew was coming.

"Raven."

"Raven?" Amber stiffened. "What was she doing at the bakery in the middle of the night? Was she at the bakery?"

"She was. Rescue workers found her and dragged her out onto the sidewalk. We were able to stabilize her and get her to the hospital in Bozeman." He held her hands tighter. "But the bakery... Honey, I'm so sorry to have to be the one to tell you this... It's gone."

"Oh, no!" Every hope and dream she'd ever had about the future came crashing down. She couldn't take a breath. The pressure in her chest was too much. Her vision telescoped in, strangling her peripheral range of view.

"I'm so sorry, honey." Shane pulled her into his arms.

Limp like a rag doll, she allowed him to drag her into his lap. He wrapped his strong arms around her, giving her something to cling to so she wouldn't drown in despair. She gripped his biceps, holding on as if her life depended on it. He slowly stroked her back in the most caring, comforting way imaginable.

Tears refused to come. Shock kept her nearly catatonic for several minutes.

It was gone. Everything she'd worked for. Everything she'd struggled to build. Her entire future became a gaping black hole of doom. How on earth was she going to provide for her son without the business?

Her gaze darted toward the hall. Joey's room was down far enough that she'd hear him before he could reach the living room. She hoped he wouldn't wake up before she could figure out a way to reassure him that everything would be okay.

"Let me get you some water." Shane slowly moved her back onto the couch before heading into the kitchen.

When he returned with a tall glass of water, she took it and gulped it down. The cotton-mouthed feeling didn't go away, but her tongue felt slightly less parched.

"It's going to be okay," Shane said. "We're going to figure this out."

"Figure what out?" she asked softly. "My business. It's gone. I worked for years simply to get it to even break. I was hoping the extra Christmas sales would give me a little bit of profit this year so I could hire someone full time. Now I don't even know if I'll be able to make rent next month. I rely on my sales for income. Without them, I have nothing."

"I'll take care of it," he said. "I've got savings that will easily cover it for a few months."

"A few months? I can't." She shook her head. "I can't take that from you. I'll have to get another job. But where? No one's hiring. I might even have to move."

"You're not moving," he said in a gruff tone. "I will move you in with me if I have to. You're not leaving Huckleberry Valley. Everyone here loves you. I—will do whatever it takes to help you rebuild."

"I do have insurance," she said. The barest flicker of hope sparked to life.

"The community will help you rebuild. You know you're going to be inundated with casseroles as soon as people wake up tomorrow and find out what happened."

"What did happen?" she asked.

"I don't know yet for sure." He averted his eyes.

"What? What aren't you telling me?"

"It might be arson."

"Arson?" Her hand trembled as she pushed a lock of hair away from her cheek.

"I could be wrong, but I thought I smelled gasoline at the scene."

"Why would anyone burn down the bakery?" As far as she knew, she didn't have any enemies. Her ex would never do anything like that, so she wouldn't even consider him for a second. He may have totally abandoned her, but he wouldn't actively try to hurt her like this.

"I don't know. The sheriff's department was on site. I'm sure they will do a full investigation."

"Do you think Raven could have had something to do with it?" she asked.

"We really don't know much about her. I don't know why she'd do something like that, but it's possible."

"Where is she now? Is she still at the hospital?" Anger roiled through her body. She didn't want to think someone she was trying to help would hurt her like this, but anything was possible.

"She's still there. Buckley and I dropped her at the ER. He took me back to my truck, and I drove straight here."

"I want to go see her."

"That's not a good idea right now. We don't know that she was involved."

"Why else would she be there in the middle of the night?" she asked.

"I don't know, but we need to let the sheriff's department do their job. We shouldn't go interview her without a deputy."

"If she burnt down the bakery, I'm going to kill her," she said fiercely.

"Hang on. Until we know what happened, let's not jump to any conclusions." He brought her hand to his lips and brushed them across her knuckles. The gentle touch instantly calmed her.

"You're right." She sighed.

"I'll be with you every step of the way. We will get through this. Okay?"

"Thank you, Shane. I don't know what I'd do without your..." She struggled to find the right word. "...friendship."

A shadow passed over his eyes, but then he smiled. "I should go home and shower. I smell like a gas station."

"I'd offer to let you shower here, but I don't have any clothes that would fit you." Her cheeks heated as an image of him naked and dripping wet popped into her head.

"Have you slept at all tonight?" he asked.

"Do I look that bad?"

"You look beautiful, as always. But you also look really tired. Get some sleep. I'll come back in a few hours, and we'll call the insurance company together." He stood and helped her to her feet.

"Thank you for coming by," she said softly.

"I wanted to be the one to tell you." He stroked her cheek. "And I meant what I said. I'm here for you however you need me."

She gave him a hug before watching him leave. She stood at the window until his truck disappeared from view.

However you need me? her bear asked in a snarky tone.

He's just trying to be helpful, she told her bear.

You should have had him help you into bed. The beast flashed a wicked grin, teeth bared.

How can you possibly be thinking about sex at a time like this? She put her hands on her hips.

Her bear shrugged but had the good sense not to respond.

She went back to bed and stared out the window. Outside, the sky lightened gradually until the orange tinge of sunrise came over the mountains. She tried to sleep, but it was pointless. She'd lost her entire life. Just thinking about everything she would have to do to rebuild sent her heart racing. She'd had to take deep breaths to calm down more than once.

She glanced at the phone on her nightstand. She considered calling her mother, who would probably be secretly thrilled by the news. It wasn't that her mother wanted her daughter to fail, but she didn't think it was normal for a woman to be on her own the way Amber was. Her mom clung to old, outdated notions about what it meant to be a mother. No, she couldn't call her.

At six a.m., her phone pinged with a text message from Shannon Wells. Her friend offered to bring her fresh eggs from the ranch.

Amber smiled.

Before she could respond, her phone pinged again. Holly and Jace were distraught on her behalf. They wanted to know if she needed them to take Joey for the day. She smiled and texted back that she appreciated their offer, but she wanted to keep Joey with her for now.

Another text message came through from Melody and Wyatt. Wyatt offered to come help her pick through what was left of the store to see if anything was salvageable, while Melody offered to cook them breakfast.

As more and more texts poured in from the people of Huckleberry Valley, Amber's heart soared. The community was rallying to come to her aid because they loved each other and took care of one another. She couldn't leave this place. Shane was right. Things were going to be hard and she couldn't begin to imagine everything she'd have to do to repair her store, but she was going to do it. She owed it to her friends, to the community, and to herself. But most of all, she owed it to Joey.

SHANE CAUGHT a few hours of shuteye before getting ready to head back to Amber's house. He'd showered before climbing into bed. After getting dressed in jeans and a rust-colored sweater, he ran his fingers through his hair. He settled his Stetson onto his head and walked out the door.

He spotted his ranch manager, Hunter Ferguson, standing next to the big red barn halfway down the gravel road. Hunter waved at Shane to get his attention, so Shane strolled over.

"Morning," the other man said.

"Morning. What's going on today?" Shane asked.

"Just got done feeding the cows. I'm re-checking the fence. I'm so sorry about leaving the gate open the other day. If Shannon tries to charge you a stud feed, just take it out of my check."

"It was a mistake. It's okay. She hasn't said anything about paying her, so don't worry about it."

"I don't think she really understands what she inherited." Hunter took his Stetson off. He wiped his forehead with the back of his grimy forearm before placing the hat back over his short black hair. "She'll be rich if she ever figures out how to manage that ranch."

"She needs a ranch manager for sure," Shane agreed. "I've tried talking to her about maybe hiring one of the guys from in town, but she's more stubborn than a mule."

"I don't think she likes admitting she has no idea what she's doing," Hunter agreed.

"Maybe you could give her a few pointers."

"If she's open to it, I'll give her some ideas on what to do. Not on your time, of course," he quickly added.

"I'm sure she'd love the help," Shane said.

"Heard about the fire this morning on the radio. Have you talked to Amber?"

"I stopped by her house on the way back from the hospital last night. Well, early this morning, really."

"Are you okay?" Hunter squinted and studied Shane as if looking for injuries.

"We had to transport Raven to the hospital."

"The new girl at the bakery?"

"Yeah. She's going to be all right as far as I know."

"Did anyone else get hurt? They didn't mention anything in the broadcast."

"I don't think anyone else was involved."

"How's Amber taking it?" Hunter asked.

"About as well as you might expect. She's upset, but I told her I'd help her through it."

"I know I shouldn't ask, but are you and her…"

"We're just friends," Shane said. Despite kissing her senseless last night, nothing had really changed with their relationship as far as he could tell. She was as skittish as a filly, and he wasn't about to rush her. For now, just being by her side would have to be enough. Besides, he wasn't looking for a relationship anyway.

"If she needs any help with anything, tell her to give me a call," Hunter said with a grin.

Shane narrowed his gaze slightly.

"Hey, now!" Hunter held up his hands. "I'm just trying to be helpful. She is single, right?"

"She has a kid," Shane ground out.

"So? She's still hot."

"Stay away from her."

"Whoa! I guess being friends with you means she

can't date anyone else. I get it." Hunter chuckled. "You'd better take her off the market before some other guy swoops in and steals her from you."

"We're not dating," Shane said, irritation coloring his tone.

"If you say so. Anyway, I've got to get out to the fences. I'm serious though, if you guys need any help with the bakery, you let me know."

"I'll do that," Shane said, although his voice said otherwise.

He glared at Hunter's back as the other man climbed onto an ATV and headed out into the snowy pasture. The thought of any other man being interested in Amber hadn't crossed his mind until now. Not that he didn't think other men could be interested. She was stunningly gorgeous. He'd just never considered losing her to someone else.

Hell, until last night, he'd never even thought she'd be interested in dating anyone. She was always working at the bakery or spending time with Joey. She didn't seem to have much time for anything else. However, now, with the bakery burnt to the ground, she'd have all the time in the world. And she was in a vulnerable place. He'd have to keep an eye out for any man looking to take advantage of her. Even though he wasn't ready to push for a relationship, he sure as hell wasn't willing to lose her.

With determination in his gait, he stomped toward his truck. Melting snow splashed away from his cowboy boots as he walked. Fortunately, there hadn't been a storm overnight, so hopefully they'd be able to walk through the bakery today to see what was salvageable, if anything.

When he reached Amber's house, the front door opened. Joey, dressed in winter pants and a heavy jacket, came running down the front porch steps. He wrapped his arms around Shane's leg and held on tight. Shane wasn't used to such a strong greeting.

"You okay, buddy?" he asked.

"Mommy said the bakery caught on fire." Joey's voice wavered.

"It did." Shane squatted down until he was eye level with the boy. "But I'm going to help your mom rebuild it."

"You are?" His eyes sparked with joy.

"Well, we need to talk to the insurance company first, but we'll figure it out." He decided not to go into a ton of detail since it would go over Joey's head anyway. The most important thing was reassuring him that everything would be okay.

"I'm glad you're my mom's friend. You can help

her." Joey grabbed his hand and tugged him toward the door.

"Is your mom okay?" Shane asked, suddenly concerned.

"She won't stop crying. I had to eat cereal out of the box."

"Without milk?" Shane gave him a questioning look.

"Yeah! It was gross."

"I'll make us something yummy for breakfast," Shane promised before really thinking it through. What if Amber didn't have much in the cupboards?

As they stepped inside, Shane spotted Amber sitting at the kitchen table. Her elbows were on the table, and her face was in her hands. Her back shook with soft sobs. His heart squeezed at the sight.

"Shane's here!" Joey announced.

"Oh." Amber quickly sat up and wiped her face with the backs of her hands.

"I heard you might need breakfast, so I'm here to whip up, well, hopefully pancakes?" His gaze darted to the cupboards.

"Top one on the right," she said.

"You want to help stir?" Shane asked Joey.

"Can we put nuts in them?"

"Nuts?" Shane gave Amber a teasing smile. "What other crazy things does your mom put in them?"

"Sometimes chocolate chips, especially on my birthday. But one time she put in coconut, which was super gross," Joey said.

"Ew." Shane winked at Amber over Joey's head. She rewarded him with a genuine smile.

"What kind of nuts do you like?" Shane asked.

"Pecans," Joey said.

"Pecans it is. Can you grab the bag, or is it up too high?" Shane asked.

"Mom keeps them in the fridge, so they don't get rotten."

"The oils in them can get rancid if you leave them out for too long. I don't use them very often so..." Her voice trailed off.

"Makes sense. I'd keep my nuts in the fridge too, but then they'd get cold and we wouldn't want that. Would we?" He arched a brow at Amber, who burst out laughing. "What?" he asked innocently.

"You're terrible."

"Only when I want to make you smile."

"You've succeeded." She stood and walked toward him. She wrapped her arms around him. "Thank you for being here."

"I said I would," Shane said softly, acutely aware of

her vulnerability. He held her close until he realized Joey was staring. He stepped back and released her. "So, how about we get these nut pancakes done?"

"Can you make mine into the mouse?" Joey asked.

"The mouse?" Shane's eyebrows drew together. He looked to Amber for help.

"It's basically two smaller circles and then a bigger circle below," Amber instructed. "I'll show you."

As she grabbed a mixing bowl from a tall cabinet, her sweater rode up just enough to reveal a tiny sliver of skin. It was the sexiest thing he'd ever seen. If they were alone, he wouldn't have been able to control his impulse to grab her and kiss every inch of her. But Joey was standing between them, anxiously waiting for breakfast.

After mixing the batter, he held the bowl down so Joey could toss chopped pecans into it. He gave Joey the spatula. The little guy grinned as he incorporated the nuts.

"Done," Joey declared.

"Awesome. Let's fire this baby up." Shane took a griddle from Amber and placed it safely on the counter, away from the edge. He didn't want the overly exuberant boy to accidentally grab it and burn himself.

As he poured the batter onto the griddle, Amber

gave him instructions on how much to pour and where. In no time, he had a perfectly shaped mouse pancake. He slid it onto the plate.

"Here you go, bud."

"Thanks, Shane. Can I have whipped cream too?"

Shane turned to Amber. "You have whipped cream? You've been holding out on me, haven't you?"

She grinned and bit the edge of her lip before getting the canister from the fridge. "Didn't know you liked it."

"It has many, many uses," Shane said in a low, sensual tone.

Joey, oblivious to everything except for the pancakes, took a seat at the table and dug into his food.

"Do you want any fancy shapes?" Shane asked Amber.

"I'm afraid of what you might come up with."

"I'll keep it PG-13. I promise." He poured a decidedly not PG-13 phallic pancake, then waited for Amber's inevitable laughter, before turning the pancake into a more mundane shape.

"Remind me never to consult you on the menu," Amber said wryly.

"But think of all the bachelorette party cookies you could make."

"Hum." She tapped her finger against her chin. "You do have a point there."

He laughed as he flipped her pancake. Being with her and Joey just felt right. For the first time, he imagined what a lazy Saturday morning with them might look like. Caught up in the fantasy, he almost burned his pancake. He quickly snapped back to the present and slid his pancake onto the plate.

As he joined them at the table, he smiled. Amber looked at him with gratitude and something more in her eyes. He wasn't sure, but he thought it might be the start of something wonderful between them. Maybe it wouldn't lead to anything, but maybe it would. And that little spark of hope brought him more happiness than he ever thought possible. Somehow, he was going to make things right with Amber's bakery, and in doing so, he might even win her heart.

9

Amber knocked on Holly and Jace's front door. She held onto Joey's mitten-covered hand. After discussing it with Shane, they'd decided it would be best to let their friends babysit today while they dealt with the aftermath of the fire. Amber had wanted to keep Joey close, but Shane had pointed out that it could be dangerous to have him on site with frayed metal and nails everywhere. He was right.

"Hey, sweetie!" Holly pushed open the screen door to let them in. "We're so excited to have you with us today."

"Where's Jace?" Joey looked past her.

"What am I, chopped liver?" Holly teased.

"Ew. Liver is gross! Mom made me eat it once."

"That's horrible." Holly winked at Amber. "Well, we won't make you eat anything like that today. Did you have breakfast?"

"Shane made pancakes," Joey said.

"Really?" Holly gave Amber a questioning look.

"He came over early this morning. I was a bit of a mess, so he made breakfast." Amber inwardly cringed. She really needed to get it together for her son's sake.

"Jace!" Joey ran past Holly into the living room.

"Come in for a minute," Holly said.

Shane pressed his hand to her lower back as they stepped into the house. The light touch made her feel so supported. It had been a long time since she'd felt like she had anyone on her side.

"Hey guys," Jace said as he rolled his wheelchair forward. "I heard about what happened. I'm so sorry."

"We're going to rebuild it like new," Shane said with conviction.

"Better than new," Amber said, trying to convince herself it was true.

"Maybe you'll finally get the extra ovens you've been dreaming about," Holly said.

"We'll see what the insurance company says." Amber sighed.

"I'll make sure you get everything you're entitled to based on your policy," Shane said. "I'll be like a bear chasing a squirrel until you get that big, fat check."

"I hope it's at least enough to rebuild what I had."

"Who's your insurance guy?" Holly asked.

"Neil Waters."

"He's a good man. He helped me get insurance on the trailer park," Holly said.

"Hopefully, he's as good at paying out as he is at signing people up," Amber said.

"If he gives you any trouble, sic your dad on him." Jace grinned.

"Not a bad idea." Amber smiled. "We'll probably be a few hours. Can you give him lunch around noon if we're not back by then?"

"Consider it done," Jace said. "I've been meaning to try my new liver recipe."

"No!" Joey's eyes went wide.

The adults laughed.

"He's kidding, sweetie," Holly said. "I'll make grilled cheese and some tomato soup. How does that sound?"

"Much better," Joey said.

"We'll be back as soon as we can," Amber said. "Thanks again, you guys."

"Anytime," Holly said.

"We're always happy to help," Jace added.

After leaving their house, Shane drove her toward downtown. The closer they got, the more her trepidation grew. Her stomach churned. Thankfully, her breakfast stayed down.

"I don't know if I'm ready for this," she admitted.

"It's probably going to be shocking at first, but we'll get through this." He reached across the truck to grasp her hand in his. The warmth of his touch soothed the chill in her fingers.

"Do you think there's anything left?"

"Based on what I saw last night, I don't think so. It was burning really hot."

"I hope none of the other stores burned down." She turned her head to look out the window. A clear blue sky and fresh white snow made the landscape look like a painting. It was almost unreal how gorgeous it was on such a terrible day. Thankfully, it wasn't snowing or dreary, which would only add to her sadness.

When they turned onto Main Street, her spine went rigid and she slid forward in her seat. She released Shane's hand and used hers to brace herself against the dashboard. Squinting, she tried to assess the damage, but the full horror of it didn't become apparent until they pulled to a stop next to a sheriff department's cruiser.

Tommy Bullock, one of the deputies, met them as they stepped out of the truck. "Morning, Amber. It's a damn shame what happened to your place. I was hoping to get a cinnamon roll today."

"I'm afraid they're a bit overdone," she said, trying to find humor in the situation.

"We're doing an investigation into the cause of the fire. Normally, I wouldn't say anything until after the fire marshal had filed his report, but I think you deserve to know what happened."

"Was it arson?" Shane asked.

Deputy Bullock eyed Shane up and down before answering. "Looks like it. Found an empty can used for holding gasoline. There are signs the fire was deliberately set."

"That's terrible. Who would want to burn the bakery down?" she asked.

"Do you have any enemies?" Bullock asked.

"No. None that I can think of."

"What about that new girl you hired?" He pulled a small notepad out of his jacket pocket and flipped it open. "Raven Beverly."

"Everly," she corrected. "Raven Everly. Honestly, I don't know much about her. She's only been working for me for a few days."

"Did you do a background check on her?" Bullock

asked.

"Not exactly. I tried calling some of her references but couldn't get through to anyone."

"You don't happen to have a copy of the application at home, do you?" he asked.

"No." She dropped her gaze to the burnt rubble where her store used to sit.

"It's okay." Bullock gave her upper arm a gentle squeeze.

Out of the corner of her eye, she saw Shane take a possessive step closer. She wasn't sure the move was warranted. The deputy had never given her any indication that he wanted to be anything but a customer.

"What are the next steps in the investigation?" Shane asked gruffly.

"I'm heading to the hospital to interview Raven."

"Is she okay?" Amber asked.

"The doctors said they were planning on releasing her later today. I need to get moving." He pulled a business card out of his shirt pocket. "If you think of anything else that might help with the investigation, please don't hesitate to call."

"I will."

After the deputy left, Shane stepped in front of her. His jaw tensed as he spoke, "I don't like that guy."

"He's harmless," Amber said.

"He can get handsy with women." Shane scowled.

"Don't go all alpha bear on me." She chuckled.

"Sorry." He looked contrite.

"Let's go see if we can find anything in this mess." She turned toward the bakery. The scent of burning rubber filled the air. Her throat swelled. She wished she'd thought to bring a handkerchief to cover her nose.

Her bear turned up her nose before settling in her chest. It put a dramatic paw over its face as if trying to hide from the smell. Melody ignored the beast as she carefully stepped past the crime scene tape and into what used to be the entrance to the bakery.

Part of the brick under the window still stood, but the glass had shattered, leaving dangerous shards poking up. Fortunately, she'd worn an old pair of work boots she'd had in the back of her closet.

She wrapped her arms across her sweater as she deliberately picked the safest path through the rubble. A partially singed cotton-candy pink booth remained. The tables had melted under the intense heat, and all the paintings on the wall were a complete loss.

As she swept some charred menus out of the way with her foot, she bumped the broken frame that had once held her business license. She'd never forgotten the day she opened the envelope to find the official document. She'd finally realized her dream of running her own bakery. Now it was gone.

She failed to hold back a sob.

Shane pulled her into his arms and whispered, "It's going to be okay."

"It's a disaster," she cried.

"We'll go to the insurance office after this. Let's see if there's anything you want to take with you before we go."

"There's nothing left."

"If you want to leave, we can go right now. But I think you should see if there's anything you want before we get a demolition crew here to clean up the debris."

"Okay." She squeezed him tighter before releasing him. He brushed her tears away with his thumb. She turned and kissed his palm. She didn't know how she'd get through this without him. He was her rock.

She took in a deep breath before continuing deeper into the mess of broken steel and melted plastic. As far as she could tell, nothing had survived.

She found the cash register lying on its side on the floor. She hit the button to open the cash drawer. It slid open with a ring.

"At least it still works," she said wryly.

"And there's money in it."

"I never keep more than twenty dollars in it overnight."

"Is all the money there?" Shane asked.

She pulled out the damp bills. Apparently, the drawer wasn't waterproof.

"It's all here," she said after counting them.

"Then it probably wasn't a robbery."

"I never have that much cash anyway. Most people pay with credit cards these days."

"We should let the sheriff's department know. It might help them narrow down the motive," Shane said.

"Well, you're right. It sure as heck wasn't robbery." She stuffed the money into the pocket of her jeans.

She walked back into the kitchen area.

"I can't salvage any of this." She picked up a dented metal mixing bowl. "The health department would declare my kitchen a disaster zone."

"You'll have to buy all new equipment. How much does your insurance cover?" Shane asked.

"I don't remember. I've had the same policy since the day I opened. I haven't looked at it in years."

"Neil will be able to tell us."

"I guess we should head over there next." Her shoulders slumped.

"Let's go see what we're dealing with," he said,

taking her hand and leading her back toward the sidewalk.

Several regular customers milled around in front of Misty's Mystical Creations, next door to her shop.

"Oh, honey, we heard what happened, but we wanted to see if you needed anything," Abigail said. She was a widow in her sixties who met with her knitting club every Friday at the bakery.

"Thank you." Amber gave her a hug. "I'm so sorry you won't be able to meet here."

"We'll find a temporary place," Uma assured her. She was another woman from the knitting club.

"It's a damn shame." Old Man Walters shook his head and slammed the end of his cane against the sidewalk for emphasis.

"I'm going to try to rebuild," Amber said.

"Soon?" Old Man Walters asked. "I can't stomach the swill they try to pass off as coffee over at the café."

"I don't know how long it will take," Amber said. Her heart ached for him. As far as she knew, he didn't have any family in town, and his best friend had passed away a few years ago. He came in every morning for his breakfast. She knew it was irrational, but she couldn't help but feel like she was letting him down.

"Well, the minute you're up and running, I'll be back," he declared.

"Thank you."

"Us too," Uma said.

"Absolutely," Abigail said.

"Thank you, guys, so much. I don't know what I'd do without you." Tears filled Amber's eyes as she watched her three customers walk toward the café. She hoped she wouldn't permanently lose any customers. She'd worked so hard to build her business. She never imagined losing the whole thing overnight.

At least she had Shane and Joey. Shane was offering so much compassion and support. She couldn't believe how amazing he was being. Without him, she didn't know if she'd have the energy to take the first steps necessary to get the bakery back up and running. His friendship meant everything to her. She couldn't afford to lose it. No matter how much she liked kissing him, she'd have to step back a bit, at least until she could put her life back together again.

Watching her pick through the remains of her dreams tore a hole in Shane's heart. He was determined to break skulls if that's what it took to make sure she got the money she needed to rebuild. Anything less than the full amount of her insurance policy would be entirely unacceptable. With that in mind, he drove them toward the insurance agency.

Mountain High Insurance Company was situated in the business center next to Huckleberry Physical Therapy. As they got out of his truck, a huge chunk of ice slid off the steep roof and landed with a thud on a growing mountain of snow.

"Ready?" he asked.

"I don't know why I'm so nervous. I pay for insurance for this exact reason."

"You hear stories about bad insurance companies, but not the good ones who actually pay on time."

"True."

He pushed open the glass door to the office and ushered her inside. A smiling receptionist looked up from her computer. Shane had met her once at the bakery when the high school's cheer team had gone there to celebrate winning a football game. He couldn't recall her name.

"Oh, Amber," the teenager bounced in her chair. "Neil was going to call you. I'm so sorry about the bakery."

"Thanks, Noel," Amber said.

"Can I get you coffee while you wait? Neil's in with someone else who was affected by the fire. I'm just glad the whole street didn't burn down."

"No coffee for me," Amber said.

"I'm good," Shane said.

"Gosh, I was so focused on my business that I didn't really look at what other businesses were lost." Amber gave Shane a forlorn look.

"The dry cleaner next door was in pretty bad shape," Shane said.

"Probably a total loss according to Neil." Noel walked over to a fancy coffee machine, popped a coffee pod into it, then pressed a button. It whirred to life.

"I wonder why someone would do something like this," Amber said.

"Someone set the fire?" Noel asked.

"Looks like it," Shane said.

"That's crazy. Nothing like that ever happens here. I wonder if there's a secret arsonist in town?" The machine hissed and spit as it filled a cup with a frothy cappuccino. Noel pulled it out. "Sure you don't want one?"

Before they could respond, the door to Neil's office opened, and Mrs. Vernon, the owner of the dry cleaners, stepped out. The middle-aged woman's eyes were red rimmed as if she'd been crying. She patted the fluff of bottle blonde hair on her head before fidgeting with her purse.

"It's tragic, isn't it?" she asked.

"It's horrible," Amber said.

"Are you going to rebuild?" Mrs. Vernon asked.

"Of course. Aren't you?"

"I'm not sure. We had a huge policy on the business, so I might just retire instead." She shrugged. "I haven't made a decision yet."

Shane studied the woman. A large insurance policy would be a good motive for arson. He couldn't imagine Mrs. Vernon as an arsonist, but she could have paid someone. Although he wasn't formally investigating the crime, he made a mental note to call the sheriff's office to mention the large policy.

"We'll take care of you either way," Neil said. Although he was only in his sixties, his back was slightly rounded, and he shuffled more than walked. He wore a three-piece suit, black with light gray pinstripes. "Amber, Shane. Please, come inside."

Mrs. Vernon chatted with Noel while they walked into Neil's office. Shane sat next to Amber. The desire to hold her hand rose up, but he didn't want to be presumptuous in front of other people. They hadn't discussed moving their relationship forward, and he wasn't going to push her either. For now, he needed to be the friend she could count on to help her through this terrible time.

"Well, the good news is that you never missed a payment." Neil sat behind his desk.

"And the bad?" Shane demanded, sitting forward in his chair.

"Actually, there's no bad news." Neil smiled. "In fact, I'm not even sure why your insurance policy is this high. It should be more than enough to rebuild. And you should have some left over too."

"How much is it?" Amber asked.

"Two million dollars."

"What?" Amber gasped.

Shane sat back in the chair. This time he did grab her hand. She interlaced her fingers with his, sending a zing of energy throughout his entire body.

"Yep." Neil tapped his computer screen. "Looks like you got it at a good price too. Must have been back around 2009 when the economy was in the trash."

"I can't believe it," Amber said.

"It will take a few days to cut the check. I'll need to get the paperwork done and get your signature, but I don't see why you wouldn't have the money before New Year's."

"Thank you so much," Amber gushed.

"I hate that your bakery burnt down, but I'm glad you were smart about your policy."

"I hate to bring this up," Shane said. "But there's talk about it possibly being an arson. Sometimes insurance doesn't cover criminal acts."

"Arson? That's the first I'm hearing about this," Neil said.

"Will it affect the policy?" Amber asked, releasing his hand and shooting Shane a murderous look.

He slinked down a bit but didn't regret asking. He didn't want her to get excited only to have the rug pulled out from under her.

"No," Neil said. "Your policy covers everything, including acts of God. This sure wasn't godly in any way, but you're covered. I hope they catch whoever did this."

"Me too." The frown on Amber's face relaxed into a smile.

The tension in Shane's body dissipated. He didn't risk reaching for her hand again. He couldn't bear the thought of her slapping it away. He'd only been trying to help.

"If you can come by tomorrow afternoon, I should have the papers drawn up." Neil stood.

"I will," Amber said.

Not, *we* will.

After leaving the office, he waited until they were in his truck with the heater on before saying anything.

"I didn't mean to make you mad in there," he said.

"Mad?" She cocked her head.

"When I asked about arson."

"Oh, that. No. It was a good question. I didn't even think to ask it. I'm glad you were with me. This whole thing is so overwhelming."

"If you want me to come with you tomorrow to sign the papers, I'd be happy to."

"You don't have to work?"

"Not until the day after Christmas. For the next five days, I'm all yours."

"I like that," she said softly.

As she leaned across the seat, her met her halfway. Her lips brushed against his in the sweetest kiss he'd ever had. It only lasted a few seconds, but it woke his bear, who let out a low rumble.

Amber laughed as she pulled away.

"Sorry about that. My bear gets hungry more often than not."

Hungry for her, his bear silently communicated.

He ignored the beast's lusty instincts and started the truck. On the way back to Wyatt and Melody's house, he wondered what the next few days would bring. Would their relationship change, or did she only need him around as moral support? He hoped she wanted more, because he sure did. He couldn't deny his attraction to her any longer. And he was starting to suspect that she might be more than just a casual fling. She might be his mate.

10

Amber didn't need to go to the insurance agency until later that afternoon. She sat at her kitchen counter, sorting through backup copies of all her bakery orders. With only a single, small oven at home, it would be impossible to fulfill them all even if she baked around the clock. But failure wasn't an option. She wouldn't let the people of Huckleberry Valley down. There had to be a way; she just needed a plan.

The doorbell rang. Joey ran out of his bedroom and down the hall. He nearly collided with her in the living room.

"I want to open it," he said. "It's Shane."

"He's not coming over for a few more hours. You

know the rules; no opening the door unless you know who it is."

"And I know they are coming over. Okay, Mom." He sighed.

She peeked out the window. Shannon's bright green eyes glittered in the morning light. Her blonde bob and wispy bangs fluttered in the breeze. When she spotted Amber, she smiled and held up a tinfoil covered casserole dish.

"Good morning," Amber said as she opened the door.

"It sure is. I brought you something for breakfast. I know it's a little late in the morning for it, so if you already ate, it heats up well." Shannon handed her the warm dish.

"Thank you so much. You didn't have to do that. Come in." Amber carried the food into the kitchen and put it into the fridge. "We did eat earlier, but I might reheat it for dinner."

"I love breakfast for dinner." Shannon took a seat at the table. She glanced down at the pile of orders. "What's all this?"

"Unfortunately, it's what I should have been working on today. Coffee?"

"Sure." Shannon picked through the sheets. A

slight frown furrowed her brow. "Wow, this is a lot. Have you started calling to cancel the orders?"

"No." Amber set a mug in front of her friend. "I've got cream and sugar if you need it."

"I'm feeling black today."

"I'm feeling blue." Amber forced a smile.

"Considering what happened to your bakery, you have every right to be upset."

"I can't cancel on everyone. They count on me. I feel like…"

"What?"

"Like I'm a part of their family in a way. Half of Huckleberry Valley is counting on me to get their holiday pies done on time. At last count, I had at least fifty pumpkin and fifty apple that needed to be ready by Christmas. It's only four days away."

"Are you sure you want to try to do this? Everyone will understand if you have to cancel. I'm sure Silas or the grocery store can get extra pies brought in. Or people can drive to Bozeman to pick some up." Shannon leaned back in her chair.

"I've tried calculating how much time it will take in my oven, but it's impossible."

"So you can do it if you had more oven space?"

"Yes, but where would I find that?" Amber asked. Agitated, she swung her foot.

"My house." Shannon grinned. "My father remodeled the kitchen before he died. I've got a large double oven and plenty of mixing bowls. I've got a stand mixer. You've probably got one here, right?"

"A small one. Not one big enough for huge batches." Amber stamped down the spark of hope in her heart. This would be an impossible task unless she had help. She hated asking for it. It made her feel weak and incompetent.

"I'm sure Holly and Melody have one each. And they'd probably be happy to help."

"They're so busy. I can't ask them." Amber shook her head slowly.

"Why not? They'd probably be thrilled to help. Everyone is devastated by what happened. People want to help you. Why not let them?" Shannon asked.

Amber sighed. She didn't want to admit the real reason behind her hesitancy.

Shannon dug her phone out of her purse. After a few taps, she hit the speaker phone button. It rang twice before Melody picked up.

"Hey, Shannon! How's it going?" she asked.

"Great! I have a favor to ask if you're not too busy."

"I'm just watching Christmas movies all day," Melody said.

"Amber needs our help." Shannon glanced at her

with a look that said, don't argue. "She has a huge pile of pie orders, and I have a double oven at my house."

"Fabulous!"

"But she needs help around the clock to get this done. Can you come over anytime in the next four days to help bake pies?" Shannon asked.

"Absolutely! What time should I come? I can start today." Melody's voice became muffled as if she were covering the phone and talking to someone else. "Wyatt says he and Jace can watch Joey at Wyatt's place. They can come pick him up whenever you're ready."

"Are you sure?" Amber asked softly.

"Of course! What should we bring? I'm guessing flour and sugar," Melody said.

"Oh, God. I didn't even think about the ingredients we'll need."

"I have a ton of flour and sugar," Shannon said. "I like to be prepared, and since I didn't know how bad winters were when I moved here, I may have over-bought what I actually need."

"I can pay you back," Amber said.

"No way. You'll be doing me a favor," Shannon said. "I've got stuff packed floor to ceiling in the root cellar. There won't be any room for summer canning next year if I don't get through some of it."

"I don't know what to say." Amber choked back tears.

"You're our friend, so we're going to take care of you. Get used to it," Shannon said.

"Exactly," Melody agreed. "Let me get the guys sorted and gather up the supplies. I can be over in about an hour, but Wyatt's already getting in the truck. He'll pick up Joey in a few minutes."

"Perfect. We'll meet you at my place," Shannon said.

"Oh, I'll call Holly too," Melody said. "I'm sure she will be excited to help."

"If she's too busy—" Amber started.

"She's too busy driving Jace crazy with her obsessive holiday decorating. Jace will be happy to have her out of the house for a few hours. And he'll be able to watch football with Wyatt and Joey. You know how the boys can be." Melody snickered.

"You guys are just..." Amber wiped a tear from her cheek.

"No crying in the kitchen," Shannon teased. "We've got work to do."

As they waited for Wyatt to arrive, Amber struggled to keep from bursting into tears. Overwhelmed by her friend's love, she couldn't stop thinking about how lucky she was to live in such an amazing small town.

People were coming together to support her in so many ways. It was a huge blessing she would never take for granted.

AMBER STOOD at the center of controlled chaos in the middle of Shannon's ridiculously huge kitchen. It was big enough for a resort. Based on the change in wood type along the walls, it seemed as if the entire room had been added on to the main house. It was almost like being back in her industrial kitchen at the bakery.

The scent of baked apples and cinnamon filled the air. Christmas carols played on an ancient record player. Holly was acting as DJ and was quick to replace the vinyl before it could start skipping. The festive music lifted Amber's spirits. Maybe she had a shot at completing all her orders after all.

Across the room from the kitchen, a Christmas tree sat next to a huge fireplace. The ovens were doing enough work to heat the place, so they hadn't bothered to start a fire. The tree's multi-colored lights twinkled in the late afternoon light. Vintage glass ornaments covered the tree. It brought back fond memories of her childhood Christmas tree.

"Where did you find all of those old ornaments?" Amber asked.

"In the attic. There is so much stuff up there. I've barely scratched the surface. One of these days I'm going to get up there and start weeding through it," Shannon said.

"If you need an extra set of hands, let me know. It's the least I can do."

"You might rethink that offer when you see how much dust is up there. It's a mess."

"You say mess, I say challenge." Amber grinned.

"Just come prepared with a painter's mask to ward off decades of dust."

"Looking forward to it."

A timer beeped. Melody set down the glass of cider she'd been sipping and pulled on oven mitts. "I've got it. Shannon, can you get the next batch ready to put in?"

"On it!"

Amber stayed out of the way as the women swapped out the cooked pies for the uncooked. After a couple of hours of working out a system, they had it down to a science. They were producing pies so quickly that Amber wasn't feeling nearly as guilty about having to leave soon. Shane was coming to pick her up to take her to the insurance company, then they planned on coming right back to continue baking.

The doorbell rang.

"I've got it!" Holly yelled.

She returned with Shane. He strolled in wearing a chocolate brown Stetson, a red and green flannel shirt, and jeans so snug they should be illegal. She tried not to drool, but damn it was hard to resist. He looked good in everything he wore, but she suspected he'd look even better without a stitch of clothing on.

"Santa's little elves have been busy," he said with a smile that melted her tingling core.

"We're already halfway through today's orders. Wyatt, Jace, and Joey went down to the café to spread the word that people could pick up their orders here," Shannon said.

"You guys are amazing, coming together like this," Shane said.

"For our bestie, we'll do whatever it takes to get her back on her feet," Melody said, pulling her into a side hug.

"I'll have your bestie back in an hour or so." Shane took Amber's hand. "Ready?"

"Let's get this over with." Her spine tightened.

Although she didn't anticipate any issues with signing the documents, she'd heard horror stories about insurance companies not paying out. Neil was a reputable insurance agent but, ultimately, he was beholden to the giant conglomerates backing the policies. Those were the people she didn't trust.

As soon as they were outside, Shane pulled her into a long, sensual hug. His body pressed against hers in all the right places. Her bear swooned and purred loud enough to be heard.

"I missed you today," he said softly.

His gaze locked with hers. Warmth flooded her body and her nipples peaked. She stroked the back of his neck, reveling in his quiet strength. As he brushed a soft kiss across her lips, she closed her eyes. Although they hadn't come to terms with their relationship yet, she didn't want to ruin the moment by bringing it up. It could wait. Kissing him couldn't.

"We're going to be late if we don't leave now," he murmured.

"Lead the way, cowboy."

She held his hand for most of the ride into town. He only pulled away when he needed two hands on the wheel to steer. So far, the catastrophic cosmic shift she'd expected if she ever dared to kiss him hadn't materialized. Their relationship was just as solid and stable as ever. In fact, he was even more supportive and involved in her life now. Maybe letting their relationship progress wouldn't be such a bad thing after all.

They met Noel at the reception desk inside the office. She was just as bouncy and perky as usual.

"Neil's in his office. He said to send you right in. I think he's going golfing soon." Noel giggled.

"In the middle of winter?" Shane asked.

"I guess. Maybe they salt the course to melt the snow?" Noel cocked her head to one side, sending her ponytail whooshing. "Anyway, he'll see you now."

"Thank you."

Neil stood up from his desk when they walked in. "Great to see you again."

"So I'm guessing it's good news?" Amber asked cautiously.

"Were you expecting anything else?" Neil looked offended.

"No. I just... you never know with insurance companies."

"I get that a lot, but I have a reputation to uphold." Neil stood straighter. "I'm a man of my word."

"Of course," Amber said, embarrassment coloring her cheeks.

"All of the forms are here. I just need some initials and a signature. I'll have the check a week from today.

I can either mail it to your house or you can come pick it up if you want it faster."

"I'll come and get it," she said.

"Excellent." Neil pointed out where she needed to sign. When she was done, he stacked the papers in a neat pile. "You're my last clients for the day so I'll walk you out."

"Noel mentioned you're going golfing," Shane said.

"Yes."

"In the snow?" Amber asked.

"Yes, it's quite fun."

"Doesn't your ball get lost?" Shane asked.

"Oh, no. We used bright orange balls in the winter. Not many people like to golf in the snow, so we get the place to ourselves. We're all shifters, so no one minds the cold."

They walked into the lobby. Noel was packing up and turning off her computer. Neil handed her the paperwork.

"Please drop these in the mail today," he said.

"Sure! Thanks for giving me the rest of the day off," Noel said.

"It's only thirty minutes. I know you have shopping you still want to do."

"Always." She beamed. "My mom's taking me to the mall in Bozeman. I can't wait."

"Have fun!" Amber said.

"Thank you. I will."

After leaving the insurance office, Amber slid into the passenger seat of Shane's truck. He cranked up the heater. Soft Christmas music flowed through the speakers, giving the space a comforting feeling.

"That went well," Amber said.

"Fast too. I don't think the others expect you back to Shannon's for a few more minutes."

"Hum…" She let a naughty smile spread across her face. "Whatever shall we do with the extra time?"

"I have an idea." He winked before driving out of town.

As they headed up the mountain, she sat back, content to be by his side. She didn't know where he was headed, but the fading afternoon light made her yearn to be close to him once more.

He parked in an overlook. A pale pink sunset colored the snowy mountains. An owl hooted in a nearby tree. Across the valley, two small brown dots, probably deer, ran alongside the partially frozen river.

"It's so beautiful here," she murmured.

"It sure is." His gaze rested on her.

"You're not even looking." She chuckled.

"I'm looking at the most beautiful thing out here." He brushed the backs of his fingers across her cheek before hooking his hand behind her neck. "Come here."

She eagerly climbed into his lap, straddling him so they were face to face. Her red hair shimmered in the sunset as it fell to curtain them. Locked in their own private world, all her cares melted away. All it took was one kiss. But it was only the beginning.

As he deepened the kiss, a soft moan escaped her lips. She slid her fingers into his hair and caressed his scalp.

"That feels so damn good," he whispered between kisses.

"You feel so damn good."

"I've fantasized about this all day." He skimmed his hands up from her hips. He walked his fingers under her sweater before skimming them across the sides of her breasts. "I want you."

"Shane." She wrapped her arms around him and held him close. His ragged breath whooshed across her neck.

"I know we said we shouldn't..." His voice was rough and brimming with desire. "But I can't help it. I need you."

"I don't want to ruin us."

"We can't ruin us." He unhooked her bra. "Nothing will ever keep me from being your friend."

"Friends don't make love."

"Sometimes they do." He gave her a teasing grin.

"Shane, I'm serious." She pressed a palm against his chest. The rapid staccato of his heart thumped against her hand.

"I'd never do anything to break us apart, but I can't deny this anymore. I've wanted you like this for a long time."

"Really?"

He nodded. His eyes darkened as the last glint of light faded behind the mountains.

"Promise we won't destroy what we have," she said.

"Never. I... I'd never let that happen."

She burned for him. Trying to deny it or to hold it back wasn't an option any longer. She couldn't lie to herself, or to him. She needed him just as desperately as he needed her. Maybe more. She'd waited a long time to give herself to anyone, but with Shane, here on a snowy mountaintop with only nature as their witness, she was ready to surrender to him completely.

11

Amber's heart thundered as Shane pulled her sweater over her head. Her bra slid down her arms, leaving her bare to him. She shivered. The intensity of being half naked, straddling the man she'd spent years resisting, was overwhelming. She couldn't catch her breath. She couldn't do anything but watch as he stripped his flannel shirt off. He was gorgeous. Perfect. Hers.

She smoothed her hands across his pecs, loving the way his nipples tightened under her touch. She dipped to nip at one taut peak before lavishing the other with her hot, wet tongue. When he groaned, she smiled against his heated flesh. Knowing she could make him just as hungry for her as she was for him gave her immense power. She reveled in it.

"You're killing me," he moaned.

She smiled coyly as she reached for his belt buckle. After a wriggling dance filled with desperate fingers and peals of laughter, they were naked.

"I've always wanted you," he confessed.

"Then take me."

She was more than ready for him. Wet and trembling, she lowered herself onto his thick, hard cock. He filled her with such excruciating slowness, then suddenly surged up, knocking the air from her lungs. She gasped, wrapping tight around him. She'd never felt anything like this before.

Throbbing with need, she pressed her cheek to his and sighed. He held her hips down so she couldn't move. Every inch of him quivered, the vibrations matching the ones currently claiming her too. She'd never felt this close to anyone. It wasn't just the proximity, or the fact that he was deeper inside her than anyone had ever been. It was something more, as if her very soul had been split open only to immediately merge with his.

"Oh, Shane!"

He moved his hips slowly, pushing her up and pulling her back to him in a rhythm made for love. She couldn't accept that she could be falling for him, but the evidence was undeniable. It wasn't just because he was making her body sing. No. There was so much more to it. She couldn't put it into words, and she didn't even try.

As he increased the intensity of his thrusts, she returned from a blissful daze. She clenched her inner muscles tight, stroking him as she rode up and down on his cock. She reclaimed control, swirling her hips and showing him what she could do.

His moans of pleasure filled the cab. The windows fogged. She loved it, because now they were truly in their own little world, removed from the harsh reality of the mess that was her life. She couldn't dwell on anything depressing as long as he was inside her. Filling her. Coaxing her toward a climax that promised to be earth shattering.

She was rushing fast toward the cliff, unable to slow down, unable to stop clinging to him. To stop crying out his name.

And then she broke open, screaming as she shook. Her body pulsed with pure ecstasy. And then he joined her with one last deep thrust. He growled as he came, filling her with molten heat. She jerked and arched against him, riding every last tremor until her muscles went slack.

She fell into him. He held her tight against his chest. Still joined, she fought the urge to sob with joy.

She needed this so much. She needed him. Consequences be dammed. She didn't care anymore. Not when she could be taken to such a magical place while in his arms.

She lay her head on his shoulder. Still breathing hard, she couldn't do anything but let him hold her. Minutes passed, but she couldn't let go. She never wanted to let go. And the thought terrified her.

As Shane slowly stroked her back, she inhaled his woodsy, masculine scent. She could picture waking up in his arms like this. A future she'd never imagined sprawled out in technicolor. Why couldn't she run toward it? Why were all her fears still holding her back?

She couldn't help but wonder what Joey would think about having Shane as his stepfather. Joey seemed to like being around him but bringing a man into their life permanently would change things, even if she tried to keep them the same. It would alter the family dynamic. She didn't care what her ex-husband thought. He'd certainly moved on and was dating someone. Why shouldn't she be able to do the same?

"You're so far away," Shane said softly.

"Just thinking." She raised herself off him and started pulling on her clothes.

"You're not regretting this, are you?" His brow furrowed.

She hated that she could do anything that could cause him pain.

"Never," she said truthfully. "I'm just doing what I do."

"Overthinking things?"

"Yeah."

"What if you just let go?" he asked gently.

"And let myself fall for you?" She swallowed back the lump in her throat.

"Are you falling for me?"

"I..."

"It's okay. You don't have to answer that." He stared at her with a puzzled look before starting to pull on his clothes. She also redressed.

When they were finished, he leaned back and lay his arm over the back of the seat. "I won't rush you, and I'm not going to use you. I wouldn't dream of it."

"It's not that."

"Talk to me. What's going on?"

"It's been a long time since I let myself care about anything but Joey."

"You can still love your son while having a life."

"Can I?" she asked with a hint of bitterness.

"According to my mother, I should be living, breathing, and serving up my soul for my son."

"That's ridiculous. Yes, you should absolutely make every effort to take care of Joey as much as you can, but you shouldn't feel deprived of your own life."

"It sounds so selfish," she muttered.

"It's selfish *not* to take care of your own needs."

"What do you mean?" She scooted closer so he could wrap his arm around her shoulders.

"How can you be truly happy when you're not allowing yourself to have what you really want?"

"And what's that?" she asked, unable to keep sarcasm from her tone.

"Love. You want to be loved. There's nothing wrong with that. You deserve to have a man who cherishes you and puts you first. Someone who can be by your side to support you and care for you and love you."

She gazed into his eyes with all the longing she kept trapped in her heart. She had let it free this evening, and the result was breathtaking and frightening at the same time. She felt swept away on a river of emotion. After keeping her head down and her heart closed for so many years, opening it again was more painful than she'd ever imagined.

"I hear what you're saying, and it make sense. But it's still scary."

"Falling in love is literally the most terrifying thing in the world." He smiled.

"And yet you seem so confident about it."

"I am. You're special, Amber. We've been together for years—"

"—as friends."

"Right. But I know you. I know who you are inside. You're passionate, loving, a great mother. And one day, you're going to make some very, very lucky man a great wife."

"Not you?"

"Are you asking me to marry you?" he asked with a grin.

"No!" She laughed.

"Okay then." He gave her a quick squeeze. "There's no need to freak out until someone's down on one knee. I'm not going to do that tonight."

"Oh." So, he would consider it?

"But maybe sometime in the way, way distant future."

"You might get sick of me by then."

He turned to her, his face serious. "Never. I could spend a thousand years with you, and I'd want a thousand more."

"Shane." She kissed him. "Don't say things like that if you don't mean them."

"You are one stubborn woman." He shook his head before starting the truck. "I never say anything to you I don't mean."

"Thank you."

"I'm glad we're clear on that, because I want you to know something."

"What?" Her heart kicked, and butterflies took flight in her belly.

"I'm falling for you. I know you're not there yet, but I'll wait. And I'll do whatever it takes to convince you that we belong together."

"Anything?"

"Anything."

"Stay with me tonight," she whispered.

"Done."

With that, he headed down the mountain toward Shannon's house. Amber stared out into the darkness. She was taking a huge leap into the unknown, but, with Shane, it didn't seem as precarious as it would with someone else. After not dating for over five years, maybe it was time to move on.

She studied Shane out of the corner of her eye. He was so confident and sexy. And so calm. She hated showing anyone the vulnerable side of herself but, with him, she couldn't hold it back. She couldn't hide from him. It didn't seem right. Because deep down, what they shared was more than just friendship. It was a connection that transcended time and space. And as overwhelming as that was, she had to smile at the possibilities. Maybe she could find love again with her best friend.

BACK AT SHANNON'S HOUSE, Shane chatted with Shannon about horses while the other ladies took direction from Amber. A dwindling pile of cooked pies covered in tinfoil sat on the counter. He'd been tasked with answering the door to customers, who had been coming in non-stop for the last two hours. They were expecting three more people, and then they'd be done for the day.

"I can't believe we got it done," Amber said, joining him and Shannon.

"Everyone worked their butts off," Shane said. "I don't have to work until after Christmas, so I'm happy to lend a hand for the next few days."

"Great!" Shannon said.

"Thank you." Amber gave him a shy smile.

They'd taken a very quick detour back to her

house after leaving the overlook so they could shower. He'd wanted her again, but she didn't want to be any later. She was afraid everyone would know what they'd been up to. He didn't think anyone noticed. They were too busy working the pie assembly line to pay attention to the time.

When the last customer left, Amber grinned. "We're done for the day. Thank you guys so much. I wouldn't have been able to do it without you."

"Our pleasure," Melody said.

"It was fun," Holly said.

"What time is everyone planning on coming by tomorrow?" Shannon asked.

"I can be here by nine a.m.," Melody said.

"Can I ride with you?" Holly asked.

"Sure."

"We'll meet you here," Shane said.

"Make sure you all take bubble baths tonight. You deserve it," Amber said.

"That would be fun. Jace and I have been meaning to try out our new tub together," Holly said.

"Is that one of the bathtubs you walk into, shut the door, then fill?" Shannon asked.

"Yep. Some old military buddies of his surprised him with it. I was in on the secret, of course," Holly said with a grin. "But you should have seen his face.

Don't ever tell him I told you, but he had tears in his eyes."

"That's so sweet that they helped him like that," Amber said.

"How are things going with his physical therapy?" Shane asked.

"Really good," Holly said. "He still has good days and bad days, but he's able to stand for longer, and he can walk a few feet. He still gets tired, but he's trying so hard to get better. I love him so much."

"Awe." Shannon gave her friend a wistful look. "I hope I get to meet someone as good as Jace one day."

"You will," Holly said confidently. "See you guys tomorrow."

After everyone had said goodbye, Shane drove Amber to Melody and Wyatt's house so they could pick up Joey. Since it was past dinnertime, Wyatt and Jace had ordered pizza. Nearly empty boxes sat on the kitchen counter.

"We've got a few left-over slices," Jace said as he rolled his wheelchair through the house. He'd survived an IED blast in Afghanistan and had come home a wounded hero.

"We had pie for dinner," Shane said.

"I want pie!" Joey hollered.

"Okay, buddy. Probably not tonight, but maybe

tomorrow if you don't eat any other junk food during the day," Shane said.

"Moooom!"

"He's right," Amber said, backing him up. "Pie is a treat, not something we eat every day."

"But we get it on Christmas, right?" Joey crossed his little arms over his chest and eyed his mother suspiciously.

"Of course, honey." Amber rested her hand on his head. "Thanks again for watching him, guys."

"Anytime," Wyatt said.

"I heard you might need us tomorrow," Jace said.

"If you don't mind. Melody, Holly, Shannon, and I were able to finish all the orders from today, but I have a whole new batch of them tomorrow."

"Drop him off anytime after eight," Jace said. "We'll be at my house tomorrow."

"Sounds good," Amber said.

"See you tomorrow," Shane said.

"Did they rope you into pie duty?" Jace asked in a teasing tone.

"Roped, rode hard, and put away wet," Shane joked.

"See, I knew those two would end up riding hard." Wyatt chuckled.

"Get your mind out of the gutter," Shane said. "Have a good night, boys."

He wrapped a protective arm around Amber while gently grabbing Joey's hand. Although Wyatt had hit the nail on the head with his comment, Shane felt the need to protect Amber from any teasing. He intended to make her life easier, not harder. Not that the guys were being malicious in any way. It was just good-natured ribbing, but Amber was still fragile right now. He didn't want anything to happen that might make her even more skittish about their relationship than she already was.

Back at Amber's house, Shane helped her tuck Joey into bed. Shane read him a bedtime story about monkeys. He tried to make it even sillier by making monkey hooting and howling noises. Amber was laughing her ass off by the time he was done.

After closing Joey's bedroom door, he went with her into the kitchen.

"I could use a nightcap," she said. "It's been a really long day."

"Sounds good to me."

"Whiskey or wine?"

"Whiskey."

He couldn't wait for her to pour their drinks. Hell, he couldn't even wait for her to grab the glasses. As she reached into the cupboard, he came up behind her and cupped her gorgeous butt.

"Shane!" She giggled.

"I've been wanting to put my hands all over your hot ass all night."

"You already had your hands all over it earlier." Her lashes lowered as she gave him a seductive smile.

"Maybe I don't want to wait for a drink," he growled before nibbling on the side of her throat.

"Are you always this horny?"

"Only when I've had really good sex. It makes me want more."

"Oh, did you come over thinking you were going to get laid tonight?" She grinned as she turned her back to him and set about making their drinks.

He placed his hands on the counter on either side of her. He pressed his rigid erection against the small of her back.

"See what you do to me?" he murmured in her ear.

"It's so hard," she whispered.

He ran his hands down the fronts of her thighs before cupping her warm center. Her jeans were already damp, and his fingers ached to stroke her where she'd want it the most. Her breath came in short pants. It was all the encouragement he needed.

He spun her around and pulled her up into a fireman's carry.

"Shane!"

"Shh! You'll wake up Joey."

She was silent until he closed her bedroom door. He'd expected a demure bedroom with muted colors. What he got was a frilly white, almost virginal, bed covered with a snowy white comforter, matching sheets, and lace edged pillows. He grinned, loving how she could surprise him despite how long they'd been friends. This was the most emasculating bed he'd ever slept in, so he wanted to dirty it up. Watching her writhe and moan while surrounded by fluff was an instant fantasy. One he intended to make come true tonight.

12

Shane forgot all about the bed the minute Amber began to strip. In a sexy tease, clearly set to music only she could hear, she slowly pulled her sweater over her head. She wore the hottest red satin bra he'd ever seen. It almost seemed wrong to take it off, but when she did, oh hell, he almost lost it.

The perfect swell of her voluptuous breasts spilled out as she let her bra slip away. She shot him a sultry look before cupping her breasts and closing her fingers over them. She swayed her hips as she rubbed her taut peaks. His cock jerked, painfully hard as a rush of blood flooded down.

"You're killing me, babe," he growled.

"So impatient." Her bubbly laughter filled the room. "Sit on the bed and be good until I'm done."

"Yes, ma'am."

He took a seat on the edge of the ruffly bed. She pranced around the room for several seconds before stopped a couple of feet in front of him. She stood with her feet spread wide, and her back to him. She shook her ass, making it jiggle in the most enticing way. His bear couldn't look away. It wanted to take her hard and rough on the floor.

"Down, boy," he hissed under his breath.

She hummed a tune he couldn't identify as she unzipped her jeans. As she pushed them down past her butt, her bright red panties caught his attention. They matched her bra. He made a mental note to spend an ungodly amount of money on more lingerie for her. If he got a seductive show like this every night, he'd be a happy man. Hell, just once a week would be a good start.

When her jeans pooled at her feet, she kicked them off. She jumped around to face him. Her breasts bounced. His hands ached to touch her, but she wasn't done yet. She hooked her thumbs in her panties.

"Should I take these off?" she asked, teasing.

"I could rip them off if you'd prefer," he said wryly.

"Not a chance. This is my favorite set."

His mouth went dry as she shimmied the satin down. A soft thatch of hair covered the vee between her thighs. He licked his lips. He hadn't tasted her yet, but he would. Tonight.

She stood before him, totally naked, totally his. He couldn't believe his luck. This gorgeous, curvy, sexy goddess wanted him in her bed. Him!

He couldn't wait any longer. He lunged forward, seizing her hips and pulling her to him. In a less than graceful slide, he dropped off the bed onto his knees.

Her musky scent filled his lungs. His belly clenched with desire as his mouth grazed her soft, silky hair.

"Shane," she whispered.

He closed his mouth over her slick heat. She whimpered and grabbed his shoulders to steady herself.

As he leisurely licked her heated flesh, she arched her hips forward. She demanded more with the insistent tug of her hands in his hair.

When he glided his tongue along her wet slit, she parted her thighs. He lashed the length of her before swirling up to capture her clit between his lips. She shivered, moaning while her knees buckled. He held her up, not allowing her to break for him. Not yet.

Lapping at her molten core, he gauged the tension

in her muscles. When she threatened to fall forward, he eased up. When she pressed harder against his mouth, he delved deeper. Her moans increased in intensity. But it wasn't enough. He wanted her screaming.

"Oh, God! Shane," she moaned.

"You like this?"

Before she could answer, he caressed her with his tongue. She threw her head back. A low wail spilled from her lips. Her breath caught. He wanted to watch so badly, but with his face between her thighs, he'd have to settle for her passionate cries.

"Please!"

"Come for me, baby."

She shattered against him, holding nothing back.

As she quaked, he grabbed the backs of her thighs and lifted her over to the bed. She lay on her back, one thigh crossed over the other. Still shivering.

He tore off two buttons trying to get his shirt off. His pants didn't stand a chance against his bear's extra strength. He tore them free, throwing them so hard against the wall a picture frame rattled. A devilish grin spread across his face.

She scooted toward the top of the bed. Lying back, she hooked her feet on the edges of the mattress. She was flexible as hell. Oh, fuck!

He couldn't tear his gaze from her luminous eyes. She held his gaze as he climbed across her body. He didn't look away as he pressed hot, wet kisses across her belly and breasts.

When he reached her lips, he groaned and slid his tongue into her mouth. He wanted all of her, to possess her like no other man could. As he thrust into her, liquid fire lapped through his veins. He sunk deep inside, finally closing his eyes and savoring how close she'd already pushed him to the edge. He dragged his tongue across hers. She dug her nails into his ass, urging him on.

Deeper. Harder. Rougher.

Possessed by a need to merge his entire body with hers, his thrusts became increasingly frenzied. He broke the kiss so he could suck on her neck. She dragged her teeth across his throat, as if daring him to bite her. He wanted to. God, he wanted to. But not yet.

Driving hard, he ravaged her. She cried out his name, clinging to him, begging for more. He'd never had sex so wild and crazed. It was because of her. He'd wanted her for so long. Now that she'd finally started looking at him as a man and not just as a friend, he needed to make up for all the time he'd lost. For all the hours and days and weeks of lovemaking he'd dreamed about but never dared to share with her.

But then it became too much. She was too warm. Too wet. Too fluid in the way she rolled her hips against his. Too all consuming.

"Fuck, Amber," he growled.

"Yes. Now!"

Her body froze. Her inner muscles clamped down hard. He grunted as his balls went tight. Then he exploded.

Wracking spasms ripped through his body. He strained every muscle in his neck as he throbbed into her over and over. And then he collapsed, near tears from the shock of how easy it had been to completely lose control with her. He'd never come like that with anyone. Ever.

As she slowly stroked the back of his damp neck, he struggled to catch his breath. It wasn't a matter of being breathless from exertion. No, it was something more. As if she'd punched him right in the heart. As if it had stopped for one interminable second. As if he had ripped a hole in the very fabric of space and time, just so he could touch her soul for a moment.

"Are you okay?" she asked softly.

His throat was too tight to speak, so he simply nodded and rolled them onto their sides. He held her like that until she closed her eyes, and her breath became rhythmic. As she slept by his side, he knew he'd never be able to let her go. In a moment of stunning clarity, he realized she was his mate. And he was prepared to do anything it took to keep her by his side the rest of his life.

THE NEXT MORNING, Amber couldn't stop grinning as she assembled the crusts for the first batch of pies. Shane had been so wild in bed last night. It was totally unexpected, but she loved it. Her cheeks hurt from smiling so much, but she just couldn't stop. Why had she waited so long to take him to bed? Sure, sex in his truck had been fun, but last night had been mind-blowing. She was shocked she could put together a coherent thought today. Getting out of bed had been pure torture, and it would be hours before she could drag him back into it.

After dropping Joey off at Jace's that morning, she and Shane had driven over to Shannon's place to start pie-mania, day two. They were all in her kitchen now. Melody, Holly, and Shannon were working on other components like the filling or the topping, while Shane was at the sink cleaning bowls for the stand mixers. They worked as a team to make sure every order would be filled on time.

When the ovens beeped, signaling they'd reached the correct temperature, Amber grabbed several pumpkin pies. She slid them into the top oven, saving the bottom for the apple pies.

"The lattice tops are done," Holly announced, grinning down at her impeccable work. The cross-crossing dough covered a heap of glistening apples.

"Great. Can you put those in the lower one?" Amber asked.

"Sure!"

As Holly added the pies, Melody finished the last batch of crumbled topping for the other apple pies.

"I don't know how anyone eats apple pie without this topping," Holly said.

"They're my personal favorite too," Shane said, fixing Amber with a panty-melting look which the others didn't seem to notice.

"Thanks for helping out today, everyone," Amber said, ignoring the pulse of desire low in her belly.

"Does this mean we get free pie?" Melody teased.

"If you help me get all of the orders done this week, I'll bake you a freezer full of pies."

"I'm in," Holly said.

"Same!" Shannon said.

"You're letting me use your house. The least I can

do is give you free pies for life. You're literally saving my reputation," Amber said.

"Everyone would have understood if you had to cancel orders," Shannon said.

"I tried to tell her that," Shane said, earning him a playful eye roll from Amber.

"I just don't want to let anyone down," she said.

"You won't. Speaking of which, I need to go get Raven's room ready," Shannon said. "She's moving in tomorrow."

"What? Really?" Amber asked. "Have you talked to her since the fire?"

"I went to see her early this morning before you guys arrived," Shannon said.

"How was she?" Shane asked.

"Good. She had some issues due to smoke inhalation, but they said she should make a full recovery."

"Did she say anything about what she was doing in the bakery that night?" Amber asked.

"I think she was sleeping there," Shannon said. "I have a feeling she's been homeless and living out of her car since she came to Huckleberry Valley."

"That explains why she didn't list an address on her job application." Amber leaned a hip against the kitchen counter and folded her arms over her chest.

"Did she tell you anything else about what

happened that night?" Shane asked. "The police think the fire was due to arson."

"Arson?" Shannon's eyes widened.

"They found a gas can on site, and it smelled like gasoline when I was there trying to save Raven," Shane said.

"Do you think she had something to do with it?" Shannon asked, looking more and more alarmed.

"I don't know. I doubt it, because she would have run, unless she was trying to kill herself," Shane said.

"Why would she try to burn down the bakery if she was homeless and needed a job? It doesn't make any sense," Amber said.

"No, it doesn't," Shannon agreed. The stiffness in her shoulders relaxed. "I think she was sleeping there because she didn't have anywhere else to go. It was really cold that night, so she probably couldn't stand staying in her car. Then someone else set the fire."

"I still don't know why anyone would want to burn down the bakery." Amber frowned.

"Maybe it was one of the other businesses," Holly offered. "Someone could have done it for the insurance money."

"Why start the fire in the bakery?" Amber asked.

"To throw the cops off," Holly said.

"That makes sense," Melody said. "Why else would anyone want to hurt you?"

"I don't know." Amber sighed.

"Your ex wouldn't be involved in something like this, would he?" Shane asked.

"No. Never. He was a terrible husband and he's a bad father, but he'd never try to destroy my business. He's not that vindictive."

"You never know with some people," Holly snapped. "Sorry. My future mother-in-law would be the type to burn down someone's business out of spite. But she wouldn't have any reason to do that to Amber."

"What if it was someone else? Someone after Raven." Shane said.

"Who would want to hurt her?" Shannon asked. A look of concern crossed her face.

"I don't know. She was mumbling something that night about how someone had found her."

"I should talk to her about it," Shannon said. "If she's in any danger, I need to know."

"She could have just been delirious," Holly said. "She was pretty much passed out, right?"

"Right," Shane confirmed.

"She probably didn't know what she was saying," Holly said.

"I hope we figure out who did it." Amber rubbed her arms, suddenly cold.

"We will, hon." Shane gave her a hug.

Over his shoulder, Amber watched Melody and Holly share an amused look at her expense. Okay, so maybe she wasn't doing the best job at keeping her relationship with Shane a secret, but was there really any reason to? He was a good guy. Everyone in town liked him. So even if gossip got out, she wouldn't have to worry about people talking. Nothing stayed a secret in town anyway. Secrets had a way of coming out.

The rest of the day passed quickly, and by nightfall they'd finished the last pie. As Shane went to the door to hand it off to the lucky customer, Amber watched him walk away.

"Not a bad view," Shannon said wryly.

"I think we might have another wedding on our hands." Holly grinned.

"We're not even close to that yet," Amber said.

"We?" Melody raised a brow. "So, there *is* a 'we'?"

"It's new, and I don't know where it's going, so please don't say anything to him when he comes back," Amber said softly.

"We won't," Melody said while giving Holly a warning look.

"What?" Holly asked innocently.

"That's the last of them." Shane rubbed his hands together as he walked into the kitchen. He stopped the second he looked up. "What?"

"I think everyone's tired," Amber said, narrowing her gaze at the other ladies, daring them to contradict her. Although she knew they were all just being playful, she didn't want to have to explain that to Shane.

"Are you still up for decorating the Christmas tree tonight?" Shane asked.

"You haven't decorated your tree yet?" Melody looked positively scandalized.

"I haven't had time. It was still in the garage until Shane helped me get it out."

All eyes swept over to him.

"We're planning on decorating it tonight. I'm sure Amber would love it if any of you wanted to come over." Shane said.

"Oh, no! I'm, uh… doing laundry," Melody said.

"And I've got a date with a new Christmas movie," Shannon said.

"I'm planning on screwing my fiancé silly," Holly said, sassy as ever. "What? I've got a new lingerie set to break in!"

"You overshare way too much," Amber said as Shane's cheeks turned pink.

"I've still got a twenty-five percent off coupon to

Lotions and Tassels if you need it," Holly said, clearly enjoying the direction the conversation was headed.

"The sex shop?" Melody asked.

"Yep. I'm on their email newsletter list, so I get discounts every week."

"Do you buy new things every week?" Shannon asked.

"Of course not." Holly chuckled. "I don't want to break Jace."

Shannon and Melody cracked up while Shane looked like he wanted to crawl under the table. Despite being ferocious in bed, he was shy, especially when they were in larger groups.

"On that note, we're going now." Amber hooked her arm through Shane's. She hurried him toward the front door.

"See you tomorrow," Shannon called.

"Have fun tonight!" Melody yelled.

"Let me know if you need that coupon!" Holly screamed as they were closing the door.

Shane laughed as soon as they were in the truck.

"They know, don't they?" he asked.

"I didn't say a word."

"I'm glad they know." He turned to her and pulled her into his arms. After a searing kiss, he let her go.

"Santa might have a present for a very naughty girl soon."

"Oh, really?" She sat back, chuckling.

"Santa just needs to find some time to get over to that store."

"If Santa needs some time off to go shopping, then he can take a break from baking pies."

"Good." He grinned. "Let's get you home before you end up on the naughty list."

"This is going to be the longest tree decorating night of my life," she grumbled, looking forward to having him in her bed again tonight.

"We've got to do it for Joey. He hasn't stopped asking about it." Shane drove toward Jace's house to pick up Joey.

"I know. I'm a terrible mother for—"

"Stop that." He grabbed her hand and held it gently. "You're a stressed, overworked mom who essentially lost her job five days before Christmas. You need to give yourself a break."

"I am a bit stressed out," she admitted.

"Tonight, I want you to sit back and watch Joey and I decorate the tree. I'll slip a little whiskey into your hot chocolate, and Joey will never know the difference."

"I've been drinking more this week than I've drunk in the last year."

"And you deserve it. Don't worry. If I think you're getting out of control, I'll say something.

"Promise?"

"Yes."

She smiled. She knew she could count on him. He always kept his promises. In all the years she'd known him, he'd never broken one. Being able to trust someone that implicitly brought her a deep sense of peace. No matter what happened between them, she'd always be able to rely on him to protect her from the doubts that cropped up from time to time.

She was a good mother. Deep down, she knew it. But it was hard to hold on to that truth when her own mother was constantly harping on her. One day she'd find a way to tell her mom to back off. But today wasn't that day. Today was a day for Christmas fun with her two favorite guys in the world. Her little boy, and the man who was quickly capturing her heart.

13

Amber laughed as she watched Shane chase Joey around the living room. Normally, she would tell her son not to run inside, but they were having so much fun. She didn't want to stop them. Seeing them together brought more happiness than she'd had in years.

After her divorce, it had just been her against the world. She'd shied away from having a relationship with anyone. She'd been too busy or too stressed to notice anyone, let alone chase after them. And she'd learned the hard way that chasing after a man didn't always yield the best outcome. This time she wasn't going to rush into anything. She wanted Shane to have to work for it a little. She wasn't just going to jump into another relationship. She planned on being far more cautious this time.

"Okay, guys. That's enough roughhousing. Are you ready to decorate the tree?" she asked.

"Yes!" Joey squealed and ran toward it. He grabbed a box of ornaments and ripped off the lid.

"Be careful," she warned. "Those are glass."

"How about I hand you the ornaments and you put them on the tree?" Shane asked.

"Okay." Joey waited until Shane handed him the first ornament. "What if I can't reach where I want to put it?"

"I'll help you, buddy." Shane riffled Joey's hair.

"Awesome!"

As Joey walked around the tree, studying it, Amber joined Shane on the carpet. She bumped her shoulder against his. He rewarded her with a dazzling smile.

"Would you like to put one on the tree?" Shane asked.

"Sure."

She chose a red and white glass ornament with concave circles in the middle. She waited until Joey had placed his ornament before hanging hers on the opposite side of the tree.

"We forgot to turn on the lights," Shane said, clicking on the multi-colored, twinkling lights.

"It looks so cool," Joey said, transfixed.

She loved the look of awe in his eyes. She wasn't sure how many years back he could remember, but she hoped he'd always remember this Christmas. It was special. So different from the last few years. She had a feeling this would be the first of many magical holidays.

The tea pot shrieked in the kitchen.

"Hot chocolate, coming right up," she said.

"Marshmallows, please," Joey said.

"Of course." She grinned before turning to Shane. "Want some extra kick in yours?"

"Just a little. It might help with the sore muscles." His devilish smile sent fresh waves of heat to her core. She knew exactly why his muscles were worn out.

After pouring three mugs of hot chocolate, she added a shot of whiskey to hers and Shane's. She dropped a small handful of marshmallows into each drink. They began melting on contact.

"Be careful." She carried them back into the living room. "It's really hot."

"Thanks, hon." Shane helped her set the mugs on the coffee table.

Joey was too excited to worry about his drink. He was too intent on decorating the tree.

While he added and rearranged ornaments, she

and Shane sat on the couch together. Shane wrapped an arm around her shoulders and pulled her close.

"Thanks for letting me be here," he whispered.

"It wouldn't be the same without you," she said truthfully.

Joey picked up a bear-shaped ornament then glanced at Amber. She wasn't sure if she should move away from Shane or not. At some point, she'd have to explain why Shane was being cuddly with her. In the past, they'd hugged in front of Joey, but it had always been a half-hug without their bodies touching.

"Are you going to hang any, Mom?" Joey asked. A slight frown furrowed his brow as he looked from her to Shane then back.

"Of course, honey." She went to where he stood and gave him a hug. The last thing she wanted to do was give him the impression that she was more interested in being with Shane. She wasn't. She loved them both, just differently.

You love him! her bear exclaimed.

She froze. Her hand hovered over the ornament box. Was she in love with him? No, it couldn't be that. Not yet. She loved him as a friend, but she wasn't ready to take the next step. She was still getting used to the idea of dating him. Not that they were formally dating. In fact, she wasn't entirely sure what they were doing, other than having toe-curling sex. Did he want more?

"Do this one." Joey lifted a snowflake ornament from the box.

"It's beautiful. Good choice," she said.

As she searched for a spot to hang it, she debated when and how she'd broach the subject of her relationship with Shane. Joey would start asking questions sooner than later, so she needed to get her story straight now.

She hung the snowflake on a branch near the top of the tree. Joey placed the last few ornaments before clapping his hands together.

"It's done!"

"It looks amazing," Shane said, but his eyes were on her, not the tree.

"This is going to be the best Christmas ever. Are you coming over on Christmas?" Joey asked Shane.

"If it's okay with your mom." Shane looked at her expectantly.

"Of course. We'd love to have you over."

"You should come Christmas Eve and stay the night," Joey said.

She glanced at her son. Did he know Shane had slept over last night? Earlier that morning, Shane had taken a shower and dressed before Joey woke up. When her son found him in the kitchen making breakfast, he'd thought Shane had come over early that morning. As far as she knew, Joey didn't realize Shane had spent the night.

"You can sleep on the couch," Joey added.

"Um..." Shane looked to her for help.

"I don't know if Santa will come if Shane's sleeping in the living room," she said.

"Of course he will come." Joey huffed. "He just waits until you're asleep. That's what grandma told me."

"That's true," Shane said, winking. "And I'm a deep sleeper. I won't wake up."

"Maybe," Amber said, not willing to commit right away.

"You don't have to decide right away," Shane said. "Christmas Eve isn't until night after tomorrow. You've got time."

"It's not that I don't want you here," she said quickly.

"Don't be mean, Mom." Joey put his hands on his hips. "Where else is he going to go? His mom and dad don't even live here."

She wasn't sure where he'd heard that information, but he said things like that from time to time that made her wonder if he was sharper than she gave him credit for.

"You're right," she said, relenting. "We'd be happy to have you come over Christmas Eve."

"I can't wait." Shane's eyes sparkled.

"It's getting late," she said. "It's time to get ready for bed."

"Can I stay up until Shane leaves?" Joey asked.

"He might be here for another hour or so. Way past your bedtime."

"Come on, Mom!"

"Nope." Shane stood. "It's time to go to sleep, bud. If you can get your pajamas on in five minutes, we'll read an extra story tonight."

Amber gave him a look of relief. Having someone to help her with Joey would be amazing. Shane often offered to babysit during the day, but he'd never been at her house at night until recently. An extra set of hands to take care of baths and getting Joey tucked in would be wonderful.

As Joey ran into his room to change, Shane pulled Amber into his arms.

"Thanks for letting me come over Christmas Eve. But... about sleeping on the couch." A sexy smile spread across his face.

"You have to at least make it look like you slept

there. I'm not ready for him to catch us in bed together."

"I know you want to go slow. I respect that. If you would rather I stay in the living room that night, I'll do it." He rubbed her upper arms. "There's no rush. Whatever happens between us doesn't have to happen immediately."

"Thank you, Shane." She sighed as he took her into his arms.

He kissed the top of her head. When she looked up, their eyes met. Any anxiety she'd been feeling dissipated. He truly cared about her. She felt it every time they touched. For her, it wasn't just about sex, and she didn't think it was that way with him either. That gave her a renewed sense of hope. It was a season of miracles and magic. Didn't she deserve a little in her life too?

When Joey called out that he was ready, she and Shane headed into his bedroom. Next to the bed sat two Christmas story books. They were Amber's favorite stories too. She picked up a book and sat in a chair next to the bed. Shane stood behind her, resting his hands lightly on her shoulders.

As she launched into the story, she couldn't help but wonder if every night could be like this. She'd wanted a family so much. Watching her marriage fall apart had been soul crushing. But maybe it was time to put that behind her and move on.

THE NEXT MORNING, Amber couldn't wait to get to Shannon's house. Raven was supposed to be moving in around noon. Although Amber had heard second-hand accounts of what happened the night of the fire, she wanted to hear the story directly from Raven. Maybe she'd be able to glean some information the police had missed. Maybe Raven would be more willing to talk to her than to a bunch of cops.

Amber bustled around Shannon's kitchen, taking pies out of the oven before putting new ones in. She didn't need to give Melody, Shannon, or Holly any direction at this point. The ladies knew exactly how to make pie from scratch using her closely guarded recipes. Although she'd hated having to share the exact ingredients that made her pies amazing, she knew her secrets were safe with her friends.

At exactly noon, the doorbell rang.

"I'll get it," Amber said.

She wiped her hands on her apron before opening the door. Raven stood on the other side. She had a duffel bag in one hand and her purse in the other. Her beat-up Ford truck sat in the driveway behind Melody and Amber's cars.

"Can I help you with your bags?" Amber asked.

"Um, this is all I have." Raven dropped her gaze to the floor. "I'm so sorry about your bakery."

"Come inside. We can talk about it while you're unpacking." Amber ushered her in before closing the door. "Your room's down the hall on the right."

"Is Shannon here?" Raven asked.

"She's in the kitchen working on pies."

"I heard she'd offered her place to you. That was so sweet of her. She seems like a really nice lady," Raven said.

"She saved my butt. I took too many holiday orders to begin with, which was why I had to hire someone this year."

Raven walked into the bedroom. Her eyes widened as she starred at the wooden log-home style bed. A teal comforter covered the plush mattress. Light gray pillows were stacked at the headboard.

"This is beautiful," Raven whispered.

"It has a bathroom too."

"What?" Raven set her bags in front of a gray dresser.

"Over here," Melody said as she walked into the connected room. "Oh, nice bathtub. I don't know what

I was expecting, but I thought it would be older. Shannon's dad must have done more remodeling than I'd thought."

"I didn't even think I'd have my own bathroom, let alone a fancy tub. It has jets in it." Raven trailed her fingers across the porcelain edge. "Once I crawl into it, I might never get out."

The way she said it raised the hair on the back of Amber's neck. She didn't know what exactly it was about her tone, but she'd have to mention it to Shannon. If anything, Raven sounded almost suicidal.

"Are you okay?" Amber asked.

"The doctors said I had smoke inhalation, but my lungs will heal. They gave me an inhaler to use, and I need to go back in a few days to do another breathing test."

"What happened that night?"

Raven sighed and sat on the edge of the bathtub. Amber leaned against the counter.

"I shouldn't have done what I did," Raven said.

Amber stiffened. Was she about to admit to arson?

"I couldn't afford the motel anymore. I was out of money. But Shannon didn't want me to move in until I had the full security deposit, which I wasn't going to have until you gave me my first check."

"You should have told me. I would have advanced you the money." Amber frowned.

"I didn't want you to think I was flaky. I'm not. I have just been going through a really rough time the last few months."

"So how did you end up in the bakery the night of the fire?"

"I left one of the windows unlocked. I waited until you were gone then I went back and opened it from outside. I climbed in with my sleeping bag. When I woke up, there was smoke everywhere. I was so confused and disoriented that they said I must have passed out." Raven's face contorted. "I almost died."

Amber felt terrible for her, but also a bit of anger. She had no right to break into the bakery. She shouldn't have been there, and Amber still wasn't convinced she hadn't started the fire.

"Shane said you told him you were sorry the night of the fire. You told him someone had 'got you'. What did you mean?"

"I don't remember that." Raven averted her gaze.

"Why would you have said it?" Amber grilled her.

"I don't know. I'm really tired. Do you need any help with the pies?" Raven rubbed her palms against her knees.

"No. We're doing fine, and you should rest."

Amber could tell Raven was holding something back but continuing to badger her would only make her shut down more. Maybe Raven really was innocent. Shane may not have heard what he thought he'd heard.

"I didn't do it," Raven called as Amber left the bathroom. She hurried after Amber. "I would never do anything like that. I appreciate you giving me a job so much. I don't know how I'm going to get another one now, but Shannon said I could at least stay for a few weeks."

"You're not fired."

"I'm not?" Raven's eyebrows shot up.

"No. I still have orders to fill, and I still need some kind of income until we rebuild the bakery. I had insurance. I can try to rent kitchen space or something in the meantime. I don't know exactly what I'm going to do yet, but we'll figure something out."

Amber felt bad for the other woman, who was clearly down on her luck in some form or another. She didn't want to add to it by firing her. Besides, Amber would need help managing the workers. As soon as she received the check, she intended to put the money to work. She already had a list of potential builders who had offered to bid on the job. As soon as she received their quotes, she'd need to sort through them to see which company could best handle everything she wanted to incorporate into the new bakery.

"I'll be ready to help first thing tomorrow," Raven said. A half-smile tugged at the corners of her lips.

"Good. We start at nine a.m. Tomorrow's going to be crazy since it's Christmas Eve. I might even start baking sooner if Shannon doesn't mind."

"Whatever time you want to start works for me. I was planning on being up at five a.m. like usual anyway so I could get used to the time."

"What kind of work did you do before?" Amber asked.

"Mostly office stuff. But I'm fine with getting up early. I promise you I'll work hard, and I won't let you down," Raven said earnestly.

"Okay. I'll text tomorrow's start time to you and Shannon later tonight."

"I'll be ready."

After leaving her to get settled, Amber walked back to the kitchen. Shannon looked up from a batch of apple pie filling.

"How'd it go?"

"Good. Apparently, she was homeless, which is why she snuck into the bakery to sleep there," Amber said.

"She's lucky she didn't get killed. Most of the time,

the smoke will kill you faster than the flames," Holly said.

"Have you treated patients who had smoke inhalation?" Amber asked.

"Not as a physical therapist, not specifically. But I have treated plenty of patients who have been in fires. She really did get lucky," Holly said.

"She's going to start working with us tomorrow," Amber said.

"Just in time," Melody said, rubbing her back.

"You're not even that pregnant yet," Holly teased.

"Tell that to my ankles." Melody lifted a foot. Her jeans rode up to reveal her swollen ankles. "If this keeps up, I'm going to have to borrow Jace's wheelchair."

"I'm sure I could wrestle up one if you really need it. Until then, you'll just have to start waddling," Holly said.

"I'm going to remember this when you're pregnant," Melody said.

"Um... so about that..." Holly grinned.

"I thought you weren't going to tell anyone for a few months," Melody said.

"I was trying to keep it a secret, but you know me. Besides, Amber pretty much already knew. I realized I might be pregnant when I was talking to her at Sweet

Cheeks," Holly said. "I had Jace take me to the drugstore. It was pink!"

"Congratulations! Am I the only one who didn't know?" Shannon sounded hurt.

"The only people who know are the people in this room, plus my parents and Jace's dad," Holly said. "We haven't told his mother yet."

"I don't blame you for not telling her," Shannon said. "I'm surprised you're even considering talking to her."

"Well, our baby will be her grandchild, as much as I hate the thought," Holly grumbled.

"She doesn't have a right to do anything but be grateful you're letting her know," Melody said, putting her hands on her hips. "As far as visiting the baby and everything else, *you* get to decide how much access she gets. If you don't want to let her spend time with the baby, then you have every right to make that choice after what she did to you and Jace."

"She tried to keep us apart," Holly told Shannon.

"Oh, no. It was way more than that. One day, when I'm not worried about getting my blood pressure up, we'll all go to lunch and tell you the gory details," Melody said.

"Yep. It's one hell of a story," Holly said.

The oven beeped.

"Back to work!" Shannon announced.

As they returned to a flurry of activity, Amber silently replayed her conversation with Raven. She couldn't wait to tell Shane and get his take on it. She'd talked all kinds of things out with him over the years. He'd always been ready to listen. It was one of his best qualities. Well, that and his naughty tongue.

She stifled a giggle and tried not to get too hot thinking about him. She'd see him when she got home. He'd stayed with Joey all day so she didn't have to burden Wyatt and Jace with more babysitting duty. Both men had offered, but she felt bad having them watch Joey so much. They deserved a day off. And Shane deserved a special treat tonight.

14

Amber pulled the edge of the sheet up to cover her naked body. Although Shane had just licked her from head to toe, amongst other things, she always felt a little self-conscious lying around in bed. Having him on top of her or under her was one thing but having him stare at her curves was another.

"I wish you wouldn't do that," Shane said, tugging at the sheet. "I love looking at you."

"Even my cinnamon buns?"

"Your what?"

"That's what I call my butt."

Shane burst out laughing.

"It's not that funny," she muttered.

"Sweetie, you're the most beautiful woman I've

ever seen. And your cinnamon buns are fluffy perfection." He gave her a lascivious smile. "I love the way they bounce when I've got you on your knees and I'm behind you."

"I wondered why you flipped me over like that." She chuckled.

"I needed my fix. I'm a man with a very serious addiction now." His tone was mock-serious.

"Maybe you need to talk to a doctor about that," she said, playing along.

"Baby, no doctor can cure what I've got."

"And what's that?" She trailed her fingers across his abs, loving the way they clenched under her touch.

"A craving for more." He pressed her back against the pillows. He grabbed her hands and pinned them over her head.

She moaned as he nibbled her collarbone and sighed when his lips met hers. Her mouth ached from sucking all over him earlier, but she ignored the soreness. Kissing him never lasted long enough. She could have done it until sunrise and still she would have wanted more.

"You know something…" he whispered against her lips. "You're my favorite obsession."

"You're obsessed with me?" She arched a brow.

"It sounded way sexier in my head." He gave her a lopsided grin.

"You're so ridiculous sometimes." She pushed him off her.

She nestled into his arms when he pulled her close.

"Tell me about today," he said.

She relayed her conversation with Raven, giving him every detail about her reactions. When she was done, she looked at him expectantly.

"It sounds like she's had a run of back luck," he said. "Do you believe her?"

"She doesn't strike me as the type of person who would burn a place down. It sounds like she needed a place to stay warm at night until Shannon let her move in. It wouldn't make sense for her to burn down the bakery. She needs the job."

"Have you heard anything new from the sheriff's department?" Shane asked.

"Nothing new. I figure they would have called if they had any more information."

"I'm sure they would have." He pulled the comforter over them.

"What happened to letting it all hang out?" she asked, ribbing him.

"You've got goosebumps. I don't want you getting too cold."

"How could I when you're so warm?" She snuggled closer.

"What's the plan for tomorrow? More pie?"

"A ton of pie. All the Christmas orders are being picked up tomorrow. I wanted Christmas off so I could spend it with Joey, not spend it slaving over a hot oven. Besides, there's no way I could handle a morning rush on Christmas."

"Are you dropping off Joey at Jace or Wyatt's tomorrow, or can I babysit again?" he asked.

"Melody's going to stay home tomorrow, and Wyatt and Jace are going to come help bake pies. Melody wants to get some 'kid practice' in so she's going to watch Joey for me."

"Can I come with you to work on pies?"

"I feel so bad taking you away from your ranch. Don't you need to go check on things?" she asked.

"Nope. My foreman is handling it. Although, I do miss my horses. We should go riding together one day. Does Joey ride?" he asked.

"He's never been on a horse. I was always too afraid of him getting bucked."

"I have the sweetest gelding. If it would be okay, we

could have Joey come with us, and he could learn to ride."

"That might be fun."

"Might be?" He looked wounded. "If you don't want him to go, that's okay too. It could just be the two of us. Or... we don't have to go at all."

"Then I'd have to find a sitter," she grumbled. "It's just that... when you have a child, he needs to come first."

"While I agree that it's important to take care of your son, you need to put yourself first sometimes. You can't always accommodate him all the time."

"You wouldn't put Joey first?" She frowned, suddenly going cold.

"Don't twist what I'm trying to say. Of course, I'd never neglect him, but if you aren't happy, how can you truly be there for him?" Shane asked softly.

"Everything I do is for him. I would never put my needs in front of his. I'm appalled you would even consider something like that. If you really want to be with me, Joey comes first."

"I don't think I'm getting my point across."

"It seems perfectly clear to me." She wiggled out of his arms and moved away from him. "I'm a package deal, Shane. If you want me, it's not just me anymore.

The day I found out I was pregnant, I started doing everything for him."

"And neglecting yourself in the process."

"Loving my son isn't about neglecting myself." Her voice rose, despite her attempts to keep it low. Joey was just down the hall, and she didn't want him to wake up. She'd have one hell of a time trying to explain why Shane was in her bed, naked.

"This isn't coming out right."

"See, this is why I don't date."

"What? Because I think you should take time for yourself? There's nothing wrong with it. You need time away from responsibility. Time to relax."

"God, you don't know anything about responsibility."

"Don't I? I work to save lives every day. Well, almost every day. On the days I'm working. I can be responsible. And I own a ranch, which I also work on. Sure, I have a foreman, but I work." He slid out of bed and pulled on his pants.

"Where are you going?" She sat up.

"I feel like you're trying to pick a fight or something. I don't know what's going on, but I resent the idea that I'm not a responsible person. I'm totally responsible," he growled.

"Shane, wait!" She jumped out of bed and walked over to where he was pulling on a sweater. "I'm sorry."

"If you don't want to date, that's fine. But don't try to make it about my inability to be responsible. My entire life is built on being responsible. People will die if I'm not responsible." He snapped his sock before tugging it onto this foot.

"I didn't mean that. I just... when you suggested getting a sitter for Joey so we could be together, it made me think about all the times my ex-husband wanted me to get rid of Joey for a night."

"Get rid of him?" Shane scowled as he put his other sock on. "All I was suggesting is that we get a few hours alone, outside of the bedroom. I didn't think it would be a big deal."

"Just stop." She grabbed his hand. "Can we just talk this out? I don't want you to storm off the way my ex used to do."

"I'm not your ex-husband, and I'm not trying to replace him. I'm not trying to be anything like him, because that's not what you need. You need someone who wants to put you first, who wants to take care of you. It's not about neglecting your son. I care about him very much, but sometimes we need to do things apart from him. It will strengthen our relationship. We can't always do that with him around. We can't have adult conversations."

"I didn't mean to compare you to my ex." She plopped on the edge of the bed and leaned forward, putting her face in her hands.

"Honey." He sat next to her. "I care about you, and I care about Joey. I don't think I should stay tonight. I'll meet you at Shannon's tomorrow morning. But tonight, I think I need to be alone. And frankly, I think you need time to consider what I'm trying to tell you. I'm not saying you should ship Joey off to the babysitter's house every day. Just once in a while. You do that because of work anyway."

"You're right. You should go." She didn't bother looking up. He just didn't get it. And how could he? He didn't have any children.

After he left, the hole in her heart grew until it became a fathomless abyss. She'd thought she could take care of her son, manage her business, and also find love, but maybe it was just a fantasy. Maybe Shane wasn't ready for fatherhood. And if that was the case, then she wasn't ready for Shane.

Shane tossed and turned until sunrise. He couldn't believe Amber could possibly think he wasn't a responsible person. Once, he'd been totally irresponsible. But that had been years ago. He'd learned his lesson. He just wished she could see him for who he really was. He wasn't just sleeping with her for fun; he was falling for her fast, and hard. And he stood by what he'd said last night. He'd seen plenty of women let their own emotional lives fall to pieces because they thought putting their children's needs in front of their own was a noble pursuit. It wasn't. That was how a woman would be slowly hollowed out, year after year, until nothing was left of her own hopes and dreams. Giving them up for her children wasn't noble. It was self-destructive. The difference was subtle, but important. But he didn't know how to explain it to her without sounding like an ass.

As he lay in bed, he listened to the roosters crowing outside. Sunlight seeped around the edges of his dark curtains. He wanted to stay in bed all day, but he'd made a commitment to help with the pies, and he was damn well going to do it.

After taking the hottest shower he could stand, he toweled off then put on fresh clothes. He stopped by the barn to check on the horses. As he went from stall to stall, he gave them carrots. They nuzzled his palm, always wanting more. He smiled. At least his animals didn't hate him.

He postponed leaving as long as he could. When he couldn't wait any longer, he got into his truck and headed over to Shannon's. Amber's truck was already parked in the driveway alongside Holly's truck and a beat-up Ford. He wasn't sure who owned the Ford, but it would be a miracle if the thing actually ran.

He took a breath before knocking on the door. Shannon opened it.

"You're just in time. We're getting the mixing bowls out, but we need another fifty-pound sack of flour from the root cellar. Can you go down and get it? We also need another twenty-five-pound bag of sugar."

"Sure."

Grateful for the temporary reprieve, he took his time walking down the stairs. The root cellar was noticeably colder than inside the house. Which made sense. Before there were refrigerators and supermarkets, people needed a cold place to store extra food for the winter.

Shelves lined the walls. Each contained several sizes of mason jars. Some held fruit while others held jams and jellies. Baskets of root vegetables took up an entire section. The apocalypse could happen, and

Shannon would never need to leave the house. Not for months, anyway.

He was impressed. His own root cellar wasn't nearly as packed. Near the end of summer, he'd made a half-assed attempt at canning some wild huckleberries which grew on the back of his property, but that was it. Next year he'd have a garden. Provided he could cut back on his paramedic hours. He'd been fully prepared to do that until his argument with Amber last night. Now he had no idea where he stood with her. Maybe he'd destroyed his chances by telling her what he really thought.

But maybe it wasn't a total loss. If she was planning on dedicating her life to Joey, she wouldn't have room in her heart for anyone else. He hated to even think it, but maybe that was part of why her ex had left.

He immediately regretted the thought. She wasn't responsible for her ex leaving. If he'd really cared about her, he would have found a way to work things out.

He sighed.

"What's taking so long?" Amber asked, standing near the top of the stairs.

"I'll be up in a minute."

"Do you need help?"

"Nope. I got it." He hauled the sack of flour over one shoulder and the sugar over the other.

"Okay, because I can take one if you need."

"I'm good."

"Shane... about last night...."

"I shouldn't have said what I said." He started up the stairs, but she blocked his path.

"After you left, I couldn't sleep. I kept thinking about our... our conversation."

He suspected she was going to say "fight" before changing her mind.

"I think I get what you were trying to tell me," she said. "I do put Joey's needs before my own. I always thought it was the right thing to do as a mother. But now I wonder."

"Don't doubt your ability. Please don't do that. I really didn't mean it that way. You're an amazing mother. I just wanted you to know that it's okay to take time for yourself. No one is going to think you're a bad mom if you want to take a day off from being a mom. You have a lot of friends who would love to have him for a few hours."

"Melody was so happy when I took him over there this morning. She's going to be a great mom." She sighed.

"You're not comparing yourself to her already, are you?"

"No. We both know I'll be the better mom. Don't let her know I said that." She smirked.

"I don't know…" He lightened his tone. "She might win the mom competition."

"What mom competition?"

"Isn't that a thing?" Shane asked, intentionally scrunching up his brow. "I thought you moms got together and voted on 'Mom of the Year' or something. You don't have a wall of trophies?" He grinned.

"I'm going to push you down the stairs and tell Shannon you tripped." Her voice was dark but her smile bright.

"Attempted murder!" he hollered. "Homicide! Help!"

Footsteps came running.

Shannon appeared at the top of the stairs. "What's going on?"

"She threatened to kill me." He nodded toward Amber, who was laughing her cinnamon buns off.

"Well, I'll help if you don't get your butt up the stairs and into the kitchen," Shannon threatened, playfully. "The ovens are ready, and we have a ton of pies to make today."

When he walked up the steps past Amber, he

stuck his tongue out. She swatted his shoulder. He chuckled.

"Hey, I know where to bury the bodies," Shannon said.

"I was wondering why you had duct tape, trash bags, and a bottle of bleach down here," Shane said.

"If you've ever wondered why I'm still single, I think you just found the answer." Shannon crossed her arms and arched a brow.

"Damn. I thought you might work me to death in the kitchen, but I never imagined I wouldn't make it out of the cellar." He reached the top step and jumped into the hall. "Whew! I made it."

"This time," Shannon snarked.

Shane laughed as he hauled the bags into the kitchen. Several mixers whirred as they beat butter into a fluffy cloud. Holly stood over them, carefully keeping an eye on their progress.

"I heard screaming down there," Holly said, glancing up. "But I don't see any blood."

"A grave, pestilent wound is gnawing through my heart as we speak," Shane said, really hamming it up. He slapped the bags on the counter before clutching at his heart. "Alas, I die." He threw the back of his hand over his forehead and started to slide to the floor.

"Oh, my, God. Get up and get to work," Amber said, shaking her head.

"Am I forgiven?" he asked.

"Depends on how many pies you can finish in an hour," Amber said.

"What's he need forgiveness for?" Holly asked.

"Nothing." Amber rolled her eyes at Shane. "He's just being a drama queen."

"Did you perform Shakespeare in high school or something?" Holly asked.

"Yes. I was the ass in A Midsummer Night's Dream," Shane said.

"Seriously?" Shannon laughed.

"Get thee to a nunnery!" he cried.

"Bruh, that was Hamlet," Wyatt said as he walked in from the hall.

"Where the heck have you been? It's been four against one in here," Shane said. "I need backup, bro!"

"Had to drop some kids off at the pool." Wyatt smirked.

"Gross!" Holly put her fingers in her ears. "Boys are gross."

Everyone laughed.

As they started working on the pies, Shane shot Amber a glance. She smiled and shook her head slowly. For now, it seemed like he might be forgiven.

They'd need to talk more for sure, but at least she wasn't actively shooting fire out of her eyes. If she'd been a dragon shifter, he would have been scorched to death last night.

And how could he really blame her? He hadn't exactly taken the best approach when he'd tried to talk to her about her needs. Hopefully, he'd find a better way to make his point in the future. For now, he'd let it go. He didn't want anything to get between them, especially not his less than stellar communication skills. She was smiling again, and that's all he ever wanted.

No, that wasn't the truth at all. He wanted her. Not as a best friend. Not as a lover. As his mate. He'd been totally heartbroken without her, and he hated the feeling. Trying to get her to see how much he truly cared for her was harder than he'd thought it would be. But he'd keep trying. Whatever else he was, he wasn't a quitter.

15

Shane couldn't wait until the last person left with their pie order. He closed Shannon's front door and walked back into the kitchen to help with cleanup. The ladies were either scrubbing mixing bowls or loading the dishwasher. Wyatt was scouring the oven with lemon-scented foam cleaner. It was a flurry of activity. Everyone wanted to get home so they could celebrate Christmas Eve with their loved ones. Shane also couldn't wait to sit by the fire with Amber and Joey. She hadn't snapped at him since she'd forgiven him, so he felt like he was back on solid ground. He hoped he wasn't reading her wrong.

"Well, that's the last of it," Amber said, wiping her hands on her apron. "I still can't believe we got everything done. I really couldn't have done it without all of your help."

"What does your bakery list look like after Christmas?" Shannon asked.

"I have some New Year's orders, but I don't need to do those until the thirtieth."

"I'm happy to come help you guys if you need it then," Wyatt said.

"Thank you. It's not nearly as many orders, thank goodness, but I'll call you and Melody if we need extra hands. I really appreciate you coming over," Amber said.

"And I appreciate your oven cleaning skills." Shannon said, opening the top oven door to reveal the sparkling interior. "If you ever want to take up house cleaning, I'd be the first to recommend you."

"I don't know about that." Wyatt chuckled. "But thanks for the compliment. I'm going to head out. Melody's got Christmas Eve dinner cooking, and I don't want to keep her waiting."

"Smart man," Shannon said.

After he left, Holly said her goodbyes and headed out. Shannon, Amber, and Shane stood together in the kitchen. He'd been looking forward to being alone with Amber again, but as the time draw nearer, tension snaked up his spine. He hoped she hadn't been putting on a happy face just because they were around her friends all day. He prayed she'd really forgiven him for last night's debacle.

"I don't have anything too crazy planned for tonight, but if you want to come over, I'd be happy to make drinks," Amber told Shannon.

"That's really sweet of you, but I'm ready to slip on my PJs and binge-watch Christmas movies. Raven went out to grab us some dinner. I didn't think either of us would feel like cooking after working all day."

"You should have told me. I would have paid for it," Amber said.

"Honestly, I would have ordered take-out regardless. I'm not the best chef. I prefer to leave it to the professionals." Shannon chuckled.

"Well, if we don't talk to you tomorrow, Merry Christmas." Amber gave her a hug.

"Have fun watching your movies," Shane said.

On the way back to Amber's house, Shane stole glances at her. She hadn't said much, which only added to his worry. He wanted to talk to her before they got there. Joey and Melody were waiting for them, so this might be his only opportunity to speak with her alone.

"Are we okay?" he asked softly.

"What do you mean?" She turned to look at him.

"Last night, things didn't end well. I shouldn't have left the way I did. We should have talked about it right then and there."

"Sometimes it's better to cool down before discussing things," she said. "I don't think I was ready to hear you."

"And now?"

"Now I think you might have a point. I always thought I had to sacrifice everything for Joey. I didn't do anything without considering his needs first. To do anything else felt neglectful."

"But you'd never shrug off the things he truly needs," he said. "You're not that type of person. You're always trying to take care of everyone else."

"It's all I know how to do."

"I think you could have more time for yourself if you wanted it. It wouldn't be hurtful to Joey. He's going to have to get used to you not being around all the time anyway. He'll be back at school soon enough. Christmas break only lasts another week or so."

"Which is why I want to spend all the time I can with him, while I can." She sighed. "I need to make up for lost time. When he's in school and I'm working, I only see him for an hour in the morning and a couple of hours at night. I feel terrible about it."

"That's normal, though. Most parents only see

their school-aged kids for an hour in the morning and a few hours at night. If that makes you a bad mother, then someone needs to tell the millions of other mothers that they're failing too."

"It sounds ridiculous when you put it that way," she said.

"Where is all this coming from anyway?" he asked.

"All what?"

"This obsession with being the perfect mother."

"I guess it started when I found out I was pregnant. When Fred and I found out we were expecting, we called my mother to tell her. I thought she would be excited. Instead, she started going on and on about how hard motherhood could be. She said she wasn't sure I was up to the task."

"Are you kidding me?" Shane jerked the wheel as his eyes snapped to hers.

"Watch out!"

He corrected the truck back into the center of the lane.

"Maybe we shouldn't talk about this while you're driving," Amber grumbled.

"Sorry. I just can't believe someone would say something like that to you."

"Well, she did."

"Unreal."

"After that, I was nervous all the time. I tried so hard not to make any mistakes, but nothing ever seemed good enough for my mother, or for Fred. They would gang up on me and criticize me for the slightest mistakes."

"That was totally unfair of them to do that to you. They should have been supportive. Raising Joey wasn't your sole responsibility. And what was Fred doing during all of this? Didn't he think he had an obligation to his own son?"

"He had very traditional views of marriage and gender roles." She picked at the seam of her jeans, near her knee.

"None of that applies anymore. This isn't the 1950s." He couldn't believe her ex had expected her to do all the work raising their son. What kind of man would shirk responsibility like that? Not a good one. That was for sure.

"Between him and my mother, you'd never guess we weren't living in the time of Stepford Wives. I even quit my job to acquiesce to their demands."

"What kind of work were you doing?" he asked.

"I was a real estate agent."

"No kidding!" He was impressed. It took a lot of persistence and personality to do that job.

"Yep. I was good at it too. Before I met Fred, I was

one of the top salespeople in our office. I was salesperson of the year when we got married. To give it up really sucked."

"I don't want this to come out wrong, but why did you let them make you quit?" he asked as gently as he could.

"Honestly? I was sick of hearing them bitch about it all the time. I just wanted them to stop harping on at me, so I gave notice at work. I did like the job, but it wasn't my dream job."

"What is your dream job?"

"The bakery."

He smiled at her wistful tone.

"I still can't believe it burned down. But I'm trying to make the best of it. At least the insurance will help me rebuild. And I'll finally get the extra ovens I've always wanted. Now that I'll have Raven working with me, I might even be able to take more orders. I've saved a little bit of money for Joey for college, but not nearly enough."

"Sweetie, he's only seven." He gently took her hand in his. "You will have plenty of time to accumulate more."

"It just feels like there's this ticking clock hanging over my head all the time." She gave his hand a soft squeeze.

"Nope." He sat up straighter and looked at the space over her head. "Don't see it."

"Oh my gosh, eyes on the road, buddy!"

He grinned, since they were at sitting at a stop sign at the turn into her neighborhood.

"Before we get home, I just want you to know that I get what you're trying to tell me. I am attempting to take more time for myself. It's just hard when I've spent seven years being guilt-ridden. Which reminds me, I should have warned you about this already, but my mother will be coming over around three tomorrow for Christmas dinner."

"I hope she's not expecting pheasant under glass," he joked as he pulled into her driveway.

"No. Just the usual. Turkey, stuffing, cranberry sauce, green beans, sweet potato casserole—"

"Who's going to bake all of that? And what army is she bringing with her?" he asked.

"I always make that for Christmas."

"Because you want to, or because she expects you to?"

"I really enjoy making all of those dishes for Christmas." A defensive note entered her voice.

"Just checking. If you're doing it because you love to eat those things, then let's make them. I'd love to help."

"Really?" Her smile warmed his heart.

"Really. If you need a hand, I'm always going to be there for you. I hope you know that," he said as he turned off the truck.

"You're so good to me."

"Because I care about you a lot, Amber. I'm trying like hell to go slow and not scare you away."

"I'm not going anywhere," she said. "Come on, let's get inside before Melody and Joey wonder if we froze to death out here."

His heart was much lighter when he stepped out into the snowy driveway than when he'd got into the truck at Shannon's house. They'd needed to have that conversation. He could feel it in his bones. All he had to do was keep talking stuff over with her. He wasn't trying to change her. He was only trying to help her relax a bit more so she could enjoy life. It was the least he could do for the woman he knew would be his mate one day.

As per tradition, Amber let Joey open one present on Christmas Eve. He stood in front of the Christmas tree and surveyed the wrapped gifts. She'd made sure to put out various shapes and sizes. The rest of his presents were hidden in the closet until "Santa" could stop by later that night. She planned on keeping that tradition alive as long as possible.

"I don't know," Joey said. He paced back and forth several times before shooting Shane a distraught look. "Which one should I pick?"

"Any one you want," Shane said.

"How about the big one with the polar bear wrapping paper?" she suggested.

"Or you could try the little one with the red bow on it," Shane said.

"Don't confuse him, or we'll be here all night," she whispered.

"Can I do both?" Joey asked, clearly seeing an opening.

"Not both. Just one. You have to save the rest until tomorrow," Amber said.

"Moooom!"

"I'm going to count to ten, and if you don't pick one by ten, it's going to be bath time and bedtime," she warned. Normally, she'd never push him to choose faster, but he'd been waffling back and forth for thirty minutes. And it was already past his bedtime.

"Okay, I'm opening…" Joey put his hand over his eyes and walked back and forth, almost knocking the tree over.

"Watch out!" Shane leapt up and grabbed the tree before it could topple into the fireplace.

"Oops." Joey flushed.

"You were pointing to this one when you ran into the tree." Shane picked up the large present with the polar bear paper, which was perfect because it was something Joey could use right away.

"Wait! Let me get the video app ready." She fumbled with her phone and pulled it up. "Okay, go!"

Joey tore into the paper. When he saw the new superhero pajamas, he screamed.

"Oh my gosh, I wanted this forever!" He pulled the long-sleeved shirt out of the box and held it to his chest. "Can I wear it tonight?"

"Yep." She ended the recording. "But first, you have to take your bath."

"Okay!" He grabbed the pajamas and raced down the hall toward the bathroom.

"I've never seen him move that fast," she whispered to Shane.

"That's one way to bribe him," he teased.

"If all it took was a little bribery, things would be so much easier. It doesn't always work out. Trust me on that. One year, I got him a toy he'd been begging me to get for six months. It was expensive, so I decided to wait until Christmas to give it to him. And you know what he did when he opened it?"

"What?"

"He cried."

"In a good way?" Shane asked.

"No. He was furious. Apparently, the toy wasn't 'cool' anymore."

Shane cracked up laughing. Amber couldn't help but smile, even if it was at her expense.

"At least I'd kept the receipt so I could exchange it for the toy he really wanted. And it was on sale after Christmas, so it ended up being a win-win situation after all."

"I hope you don't do that too often. You don't want to spoil him," Shane warned.

"No. That was the only time. Normally, he's very grateful. He's a good kid. He really doesn't ask for much, so when he does want something, I try to get it for him if I can afford it."

Shane's smile widened.

"What?" she asked.

"See, that's something a good mom would do."

"Please tell me you're not judging me too." Her mouth tightened.

"No. Not at all. I wouldn't dream of it. What do I know about raising kids anyway? You're an expert compared to me."

"There's no manual. You just have to figure it out as you go," she said.

"No manual means no scoring system. See, nothing to worry about." He moved closer and slid his hands down her back to rest on her butt.

"We need to go back there before he tries to start the bath without us." She gave him a quick kiss. "But save that thought for later, okay?"

"Oh, baby!"

She laughed as she headed toward the bathroom, realizing Shane was just as clueless about raising kids as she was. They would make one hell of a team. The blind leading the blind. But at least they'd have each other to bounce ideas off. It was more than she had right now. Rather than help her, her mother chose to criticize. So she was no help.

"Is there any bubble bath?" Shane asked as they walked into the bathroom.

"Fluffy Bubbles!" Joey grabbed a bright blue bottle and handed it to him.

"Is it okay?" Shane asked her.

"Sure." Normally, she reserved bubbles for the weekend when she had more time to spend waiting on him to finish with his bath.

"Can I have Mr. Ducky too?" Joey asked.

"This guy?" Shane grabbed a big, yellow, rubber duck.

"That's him!"

"Oh, no! Mr. Ducky's jumping in." Shane made a whistling sound as he plunged the toy into the bathtub. The duck disappeared under the bubbles.

Joey quickly jumped in. Water sloshed over the side.

"I'll grab a towel," Shane said.

"Hall closet. Thank you."

"Shane's cool," Joey said as soon as Shane left the room.

"Yep. I like him a lot too."

"Is he staying the night like he said?"

"Yes. He'll be sleeping on the couch," she said, feeling the need to reinforce that idea.

"Okay. As long as he won't scare Santa away."

"I might growl at him when he comes down the chimney." Shane roared as he walked back into the room.

"NO!" Joey's eyes went wide, and his bottom lip trembled.

"I'm just kidding, bud. I wouldn't ever do something like that." He knelt by the tub and lay the towel across the spilled water.

Sufficiently placated, Joey resumed playing with

his toy until the bubbles all popped and the water went cold. Amber toweled him off while Shane waited for them in Joey's room. After tucking her son into bed, she read the first bedtime story to him. Shane read the second. And soon, Joey was asleep.

She stood next to Shane, who wrapped his arm around her waist. They watched her son sleep for several minutes without speaking. It just felt right. Like everything else when she was with Shane. She could see every night being just like this, minus the Christmas presents and bubbles, of course. Every night couldn't be Christmas Eve, no matter how much she wished it were so.

16

Christmas morning started with slow, sensual sex with Shane. Amber didn't want to let him out of her bed, but he couldn't be there when Joey woke up. She rolled onto her side and gazed at Shane's sleeping form. He was everything she ever wanted in bed. He was her best friend. And now, she was certain she wanted to see where they could take their relationship. So far, they'd been dancing around labeling it, but now she wanted to be his girlfriend. It seemed like such a silly word. What she felt for him was so much deeper. But what else could she call herself now?

"Do you think we have time for another roll around?" Shane asked sleepily. He wrapped his arms around her and pulled her in for a kiss.

"It's almost sunrise. Joey will wake up as soon as it gets light enough. As much as I want to keep you in here all day, I can't." She pouted her lips.

"I feel like I'm a teenager again, sneaking around."

"It's only for a little while. Until we figure things out."

"What's there to think about? You know you mean the world to me, don't you?" he asked.

"And I care about you a lot too," she said.

"Tell me what more I need to do to convince you we belong together."

"I don't... It just... Shane." She couldn't get past her shock. He'd implied that he wanted to be with her before, but he'd never said it so clearly.

"I'm falling in love with you." Shane pushed a lock of her hair away from her face. "I think I've felt this way for a really long time."

"I care about you too."

"You just said that. But caring about someone isn't the same as loving them," he said softly.

"No. It's not. And I get the difference. It's just... this whole time I went along with what we were doing because it felt right."

"Because we belong together."

"I thought the same thing with my ex." She pulled

the blanket up to her neck. "And that was a huge mistake."

"You're afraid of messing up again."

"It's more than that. I need to think about Joey. It's not about trying to put him first all the time," she quickly added.

"Then how does he factor into our relationship? I consider you two a package deal. He's the sweetest kid, and we get along great. You must be able to see that," he said.

"I do." He was right about that. Joey practically worshiped Shane.

"Then what's the problem?" he asked.

"When you've been hurt the way I was hurt, it's hard to give someone your heart again." It was the truth, but somehow felt humiliating to admit.

"So, you've been holding back?"

"No. I haven't been able to stop this thing between us. Trust me, before we started getting intimate, I tried like hell never to think about you as anything other than my friend."

"I know what you mean. I did whatever it took not to think about you when you weren't around, but I couldn't stop myself."

"You thought about me, like that? Before we got together?" She couldn't believe he'd kept his feelings a secret for so long. But then again, if he'd tried to get her to date him earlier in their relationship, she would have run like hell to get away. She hadn't been ready then. But was she ready now?

"Amber, ever since we met, all I could think about was how much I loved being around you. It started as friendship, but over the years, it's becoming something else. Something more. It got to the point where I just couldn't hold back any longer. And I don't want to deny what I feel anymore. I told you I was falling in love with you, but that's not exactly true either. I love you. I love you with all my heart and with everything I am. If you need more time, I'll give it to you. But I don't need more time, because I already know what's in my heart." His fingers laced between hers. When he closed his hand around hers, she held his too.

She didn't know what to say. He loved her. It was unreal. A fantasy come true. She wasn't sure she even deserved his love. She'd been denying what her heart had been telling her all along. He was her mate.

"Shane, I lo—"

"Mooom! Santa came!" Joey shrieked just outside her door.

"Oh crap." Amber pulled the covers over her head. "What do we do now?"

"I'll go hide in the bathroom. Get dressed. If you

can distract him for a few minutes, I'll sneak out the window. I'll bring some firewood in from outside. He'll think I was out there the whole time."

"Okay, be careful," she whispered to Shane before raising her voice so Joey could hear her. "Coming, honey!"

"Santa left so many presents. Can I open one? Can I?" Joey asked.

"Just a second."

She hopped out of bed and pulled on a lounge sweater and leggings. Shane grabbed his clothes before heading into the bathroom. He closed the door softly. She smiled. She wanted to savor what he'd told her, but she couldn't dawdle, or Joey would have all the presents unwrapped.

When she opened the door, the hall was empty. She walked into the living room to find Joey sitting on the floor. He held a box gift wrapped with a reindeer design. He'd already pulled the red ribbon free, but he hadn't torn the paper.

"Good job waiting," she said. "Open that one and then give me a minute to make coffee, okay?"

"Yay!"

As Joey tore into the package, Amber tried to listen for Shane. So far Joey hadn't seemed to notice that Shane wasn't with them.

"Oh my God! I've wanted this forever!" Joey held up a remote-controlled sports car. "Can I play with it now?"

"Sure." She popped open the back of the toy to check for batteries. "Oh, wait, I need to grab some batteries."

She went to the junk drawer in the kitchen and dug around until she found a set.

You won't be needing those anymore, her bear snarked.

Amber burst out laughing. The beast was right. Ever since Amber had welcomed Shane into her bed, she hadn't felt the need to play with her adult toys.

She popped the batteries into the car and handed it to her son.

"Just don't run it too fast. I don't want you breaking it today," she warned.

"Vroom, vroom!" He used the controls to race the car across the kitchen floor toward the back door.

As the door opened, she gasped. Shane held a pile of firewood at chest height, but there was no way he'd be able to see over it to see the car.

"Look out!" she yelled.

"Ahh!" Joey screamed as he frantically hit the control buttons.

The car sped under Shane's raised foot, then slammed into his other ankle.

"Ouch! What was that?"

"My new car," Joey said. "Sorry, I didn't know you were outside."

"I went to grab more firewood." He winked at Amber as he walked past her.

"I'm making coffee. Want any?"

"A whole pot if you have it," Shane said.

"Did you sleep bad on the couch?" Joey asked.

"Yep." Shane set the firewood in a pile near the fireplace. He placed a few logs inside and lit it. Soon a crackling fire flickered, adding to the warmth of the Christmas scene.

"Maybe we should save the car for later when we can go outside," Amber said.

"No! I want to play with it now!"

"Listen to your mom," Shane said. "We don't want to break anything in the house."

"Fine." Joey took the car into the living room and dropped it on the coffee table. "Can I open another one?"

"Coffee's almost ready," Amber said.

After fixing herself a mug with cream and sugar, she handed Shane a cup of black coffee.

"You're an angel," he said.

"Good job getting the firewood." She grinned over the rim of her cup.

"Oh, I've got all kinds of wood ready for you." He waggled his eyebrows.

She laughed so hard she almost shot coffee out her nose.

"Wow, say it, don't spray it!" Shane backed up but was still smiling.

"Just for that, you're on breakfast duty."

"Pancakes?" he asked.

"And eggs, and maybe some bacon. I'm so hungry."

"I wonder why," he teased.

She laughed and swatted him on the butt before heading into the living room. She sat on the couch while Joey unwrapped presents from "Santa". He was getting older now and they wouldn't have many more Christmases before he'd discover the truth. She wanted to enjoy this time as much as possible.

The scent of bacon filled the air. A few minutes later, Shane brought three plates into the room. His and hers were piled with food, while Joey's portion was much more reasonable.

As the pile of presents dwindled and wrapping paper cluttered the living room, Amber leaned against Shane. She'd had plenty of Christmas mornings with her ex, but she'd never felt like it was more than a formality. Shane seemed truly involved with Joey, commenting on his presents and helping him unwrap the boxes with tightly knotted bows. It was perfect.

When Joey reached a handful of presents that hadn't been wrapped by her, she quirked a brow at Shane. He grinned.

Joey unwrapped the first gift, which was a child-sized black Stetson cowboy hat. He squealed with delight.

"Now I'm a real man!" He shoved the hat onto his head. It was slightly big, falling to cover his eyes. He pushed it up and angled it so it wouldn't fall again.

"You look like the fiercest cowboy in the West," Shane said in a cowboy drawl. He sounded a bit like John Wayne.

"You have a few more presents to open," Amber said. She glanced at her watch. She'd have to get started with cooking soon.

The next gift puzzled Joey. He pulled a western horse bridle out of the box.

"That's for when we go riding," Shane said.

"I can't wait! Mom never lets me go. She says it's too dangerous."

"Well, that's no fun." Shane winked at her. "I've got to work tomorrow, but how about you come over the day after and we'll go riding?"

"Yay!"

"Shane, we didn't discuss this first." She pressed her lips into a thin line. She still wasn't convinced that Joey would be safe. All kinds of things could go wrong.

"I'm sorry. I thought we decided it would be okay for him to ride. I wouldn't have offered otherwise." Shane rubbed her back, but the tension knotted there wouldn't go away.

"I just don't think it's a good idea yet. He's so little, and if the horse kicks—"

"Nothing's going to happen. I promise." He gave her one of his dazzling smiles.

"Okay. But he'd better not get hurt."

"I won't, Mom!"

Joey tore into the next gift, revealing a brown leather western horse saddle. The last gift was a pair of cowboy boots.

"Can I wear them now?" he asked.

"If you change into clothes, you can wear them. Grandma will be over in a couple of hours. Shane and I need to start cooking. We have a few Christmas movies you can watch while you play with your toys."

"Can I go outside with my car?"

"Not yet. Wait until one of us can go out there with you," she said.

"Fine." He pouted for a second before running down the hall to his bedroom.

"Shane, I wish you would have asked me first." She stood and walked toward the kitchen.

"I didn't think you'd be upset by it." He followed her. "If you want, I can take the stuff back and get him something else."

"No. It's too late now. You can't take gifts away from kids."

"That would make me a monster, wouldn't it?" Shane grinned.

"Yes, it would." She chuckled. "I'm probably just overthinking the whole riding thing."

"You are, but I still love you anyway."

There it was again, that word. Love. She'd been about to tell him that she loved him too before they'd been interrupted. Now, it didn't seem like the right time. Maybe it would be better to wait until later tonight.

THREE HOURS LATER, Amber pulled a bubbling sweet potato casserole out of the oven. She closed the door with her hip before placing the dish on a trivet. She leaned over Shane's shoulder to watch him sprinkle toasted sliced almonds over a tray of lightly sautéed green beans.

"A little more," she instructed.

"You say that in and out of the bedroom," he whispered wickedly, turning to take her into his arms.

"You're so dirty!" She glanced toward the living room. Joey sat in front of the television, watching a cartoon movie with snowmen. He was oblivious to the adult conversation.

"Wait until tonight." Shane pulled her against his hard chest.

"What's happening tonight?" she asked, far too innocently.

The doorbell rang.

"Oh, God! She's early!"

Amber went into total panic mode. The turkey wouldn't be done for at least another twenty minutes. Thankfully, Shane had created a charcuterie board. Shaped like a Christmas tree, the snacks included a variety of hard and soft cheeses, green and red grapes, artfully folded Calabrese salami and Soppressata, and star-shaped Provolone.

"Calm down, honey," Shane started.

"Calm down? Nothing's ready yet!"

"The wine's ready, and that's all we'll need right now. In fact, have a glass while I get the door."

She took his advice and popped open a bottle of Cabernet Sauvignon. She poured herself a huge glass and gulped half of it before her mom walked into the kitchen.

"It smells divine in here," she said as she gave Amber a hug. "But, oh, you should have waited a bit before putting the marshmallows on the sweet potatoes. They're going to melt."

"I like mine melted," Shane said, coming to Amber's defense.

"Me too." Amber raised her chin slightly.

"Well, anyway, I'm sure it will still taste good." Her mom opened the cupboard and pulled out a wine glass. "Normally, I wouldn't start drinking before food, but since it's not ready…"

"It's almost done," Shane said. "And, we have a charcuterie tray ready. Would you like to take it into the living room? I'm sure Joey will be hungry by now."

"Didn't you feed him lunch?" Her mom frowned, eyeing Shane. "When did you arrive?"

"Earlier." Shane smiled sweetly in that don't-question-me kind of way.

"How very sweet of you to come and help her. Does that mean you're dating now?" Her mom poured a full glass of Cabernet Sauvignon.

Shane looked to Amber for help. She smiled as if to say, 'I've got this'.

"We are dating," Amber said, lowering her voice. "But we haven't talked to Joey about it yet. So please don't bring it up. I don't want to have to explain it all to him today."

"Is it serious?" her mom asked.

Amber didn't know how to respond to that. Thankfully, Shane stepped in.

"As serious as burnt turkey. Should we check it again?"

"Oh, yes. Right now." Amber pulled open the oven and resisted the urge to climb into it. She hadn't considered telling her mother about Shane yet, but she'd felt pushed into a corner, as usual.

"It looks perfect." Shane slipped a pair of oven mitts on and heaved the huge turkey out. "Where do you want it?"

"On the table, please." Amber had already set the table with Christmas dishes she'd ordered online. The design depicted adorable blue and white polar bears playing in a snowy village. She'd added a couple of tapered red candles to the center, flanking the festive pine and holly centerpiece.

"We should let it rest for twenty to thirty minutes," Shane said.

"Smart man you've got here." Her mother practically swooned over him.

Amber stamped down a rush of jealousy. Her mother never had anything but criticism for her. Yet, Shane could do no wrong in her eyes. It was annoying, but at least she liked Shane. Christmas would have been a nightmare if she hated him.

"Shall we sit in the living room?" her mother asked.

"Please. I'll bring over some appetizer plates and napkins."

After her mother left the kitchen, Shane whispered, "Relax."

"She's always so critical with me," Amber complained.

"Just because someone's snippy doesn't mean you have to believe what they think about you. I'm sure she's not perfect either, so she shouldn't expect you to be." Shane ran his hand down Amber's arm. "Come on, honey. Let's go stuff our faces and watch cartoons all day."

She smiled and gave Shane a quick hug. He always made everything better, even tense exchanges with her mother. For once, her mom was right about one thing: Shane was a keeper.

17

Shane sat back in the chair and covered his belly with his hand. He hadn't eaten that much for Christmas in years. In the past, he'd always volunteered to work on holidays so the guys with families could have those days off. He'd felt a bit guilty about taking the time this year, but as he watched Amber play with Joey, he knew he'd made the right decision.

"How are you with kids?" Amber's mom asked. She sat beside him on the sofa.

"Good. I think." *What an odd question.*

"Are you planning on having more?" she asked.

"Mother!" Amber turned to face her mother. She narrowed her gaze. "I already told you we're not talking about that right now."

"Why not? You're going to have to figure details like that out. Might as well do it before you get married," Blythe reasoned.

"Are you getting married?" Joey set his toy down. His gaze jumped from his mom, to his grandmother, before landing on Shane.

"No. Not... No." Amber bit her bottom lip.

"Are you going to be my dad?" Joey stared at him intently.

"Um..." Shane had no idea how to answer. He didn't want to overstep his boundaries. He wanted more than anything to be Joey's stepfather, but Amber was already mad about the horseback riding situation. He didn't dare presume anything at this point.

"Why's everyone look so weird?" Joey asked.

"Sometimes we don't know the answer to questions yet. And we need time to think about it," Amber said.

"Well, I don't have to think about it." Joey ran over and wrapped his arms as far as they would go around Shane's body. "I want you to be my dad. It would be the best Christmas present ever. Then the kids at school will stop asking me if I have a dad."

"You do have a dad. He's in New York," Blythe said, unhelpful as always. "Shane would be your stepdad."

"Nate at school has a stepdad. He's cool," Joey said.

"Thanks, Mother," Amber snarled under her breath.

"You know I'm just trying to help. Anyway, I should be going. I promised Vivian I'd stop by the country club for her wine and cheese Christmas evening reception. It's terrible her family didn't invite her to Christmas. Just because she's getting a divorce doesn't mean she's not part of the family any longer." Blythe huffed.

"She was invited to Charles's new house for Christmas, but she chose not to go," Amber said. "I don't know how she could ignore her own children like that."

"I'm sure she has her reasons if what you say is even true. You know how it is with the gossips in Huckleberry Valley. Sometimes it's hard to separate the truth from the lies." Blythe walked to the front door. She pulled on her winter jacket and snow gloves.

"Drive safe," Amber said, giving her mom a hug.

"If you get engaged, I'd like to be the first to know," Blythe said. "And just so you know, Shane, you already have my blessing. She's needed a new man in her life for a long time. It's not right that she's all alone."

"Okay, Mom. Goodnight." Amber opened the front

door. A blast of cold air rushed in. After closing it, she shook her head softly. "She's always such fun to have around."

"Seems like it. But you heard what she said, I've got her blessing." He grinned, trying to lighten the mood.

"Don't make me kick you out," she threatened. The edges of her lips quirked up.

"You can't even say it with a straight face." He chuckled.

"Mom, is Shane going to be my new dad?" Joey asked. He sat under the Christmas tree but hadn't resumed playing with his toys. The concern on his face tore at Shane's heart.

"Shane and I care about each other a lot," Amber said. She glanced at him before continuing. "But we still have a lot to think about first."

"Like what? I want a dad," Joey pouted.

"Adult things," Shane said. "But don't worry. We both love you very much."

He wasn't sure if he was overstepping by telling Joey how he felt, but Shane didn't want him to be scared or upset.

"Let's pick a new Christmas movie. Something short. I'll bring over a tray of cookies," Amber said.

"Cookies?" Joey's eyes lit up.

Sweet-Talking Cowbear

"You can pick two. We'll watch the movie, and then it's bedtime. Okay?" Amber asked.

"I want a gingerbread and a Christmas angel cookie."

"Coming right up." Amber smiled at her son before giving Shane a relieved look. Too bad everything wrong with the world couldn't be solved with cookie bribery.

"Let's see what we've got for movies," Shane said.

As Joey gave him several options and explained the benefits of each one, Shane wasn't really listening. He kept thinking about Amber's reaction to her mother's totally inappropriate questions. Amber hadn't seemed too excited by the prospect of getting married. Not that Shane had even considered asking her yet. She was already so skittish he didn't want to risk pushing her away. Maybe if she could see how good he was with Joey, she would be more open to moving their relationship to the next level. He'd have to make sure Joey had an extra good time when they went horseback riding.

He smiled as Amber returned with the cookies. She was gorgeous in her simple red sweater and black leggings. Her fiery red hair hung in curls around her face. She hadn't put it up today the way she normally did. He loved it down but understood why she couldn't do that while she was at work. Later, he planned on running his fingers through those silky locks.

"Want a cookie?" Amber asked him as she placed the tray on the coffee table.

"There's only one cookie I want right now." He gave her a pointed look.

"Well, the only ones I have available until after bedtime are right here." She plucked up a gingerbread man and snapped its head off.

"Ouch."

"Well, it's the only thing I can maim right now."

"We're going to watch this one," Joey said, thrusting a movie toward Shane.

"I haven't seen that one," Shane said, studying the cartoon characters on the cover. "Looks great."

"It's the best one ever." Joey leaned down and placed his hands on the coffee table. He studied the available treats as if this were the most important decision of his life. "Okay, this one..." He grabbed a sugar cookie angel. "And this one!" He grabbed the last gingerbread man.

They sat in silence while the film played. Amber sat so close to Shane he could feel her warmth seeping into his skin. He wrapped an arm around her and pulled her against his side. She looked up at him with a sexy smile. God, he couldn't wait to get her alone later.

When the movie ended, Joey yawned.

"Time to get ready for bed," Amber announced.

"Is Shane going to be here tomorrow?"

"No, I've got to work. But we'll go horseback riding the day after that. Okay?" Shane asked.

"I guess."

"Let's go. You can take a quick bath then get your new PJs on," Amber said.

After Joey left for the bathroom, she turned to Shane. "I'm so tired I think I could fall asleep on the couch."

"Not a chance. You're all mine tonight."

"We have to wait until he's asleep."

"After all the excitement today, I'm sure he will be out like a light."

"Me too. I'll go check on him," she said.

"I'll clean up while you do."

As she took care of getting Joey ready for bed, Shane cleaned the kitchen. Other than the small snafu with Amber's mother, the day had been perfect.

He smiled as he scrubbed the mashed potato pot. This was it. What he'd always wanted. A gorgeous wife, a cute kid. He'd just been too afraid to really go after her. Now he wished he hadn't wasted so many years. If only he'd been more aggressive.

Should have listened to me the first time I told you she was our mate, his bear snarked.

I hadn't known her that long, Shane reasoned.

Long enough. One look and I knew she was our mate.

We've had this argument before.

All you have to do is tell me I'm right. His bear dragged a sharp claw across Shane's ribs.

"Stop that!" Shane growled.

"Stop what?" Amber asked, walking into the kitchen.

"Just having a strongly worded discussion with my bear."

"Like a fight?" She smirked.

"No," he scoffed. "My bear listens to me."

"Sure he does." She poured herself a glass of wine.

"Doesn't your bear listen to you?"

"Ha! She's got a mind of her own."

"Mine drives me crazy if I don't let him out to run around."

"When was the last time you shifted?" she asked.

"It's been a while."

"We should go outside and run around for a few minutes."

"What about Joey?" he asked.

"Baby monitor." She held up her phone and wiggled it. "There's an app for everything these days."

"How are you going to hold it when you're shifted?" It wasn't that he was against the idea, he just wanted to make sure Joey would be safe.

"I have a clip-on adjustable arm for when I'm using my phone hands free in the car. I can attach it to a tree. He'll be fine. He's asleep and won't wake up until morning. He never gets up in the middle of the night."

"If you're sure about this and you're positive he'll be safe, then we can do it."

"You're starting to sound like me," she teased.

"Maybe I'll turn into an overprotective dad."

"Maybe."

Her glowing smile gave him a rush of hope. Things were going to work out between them. He felt it in his soul.

AMBER DOUBLE-CHECKED her phone to make sure it was tightly affixed to the tree branch. She didn't plan on going far, just in case anything happened. She could quickly shift back into her human form if necessary, although she highly doubted she'd need to. Joey had been sleeping through the night for years. She didn't think he'd wake up tonight.

"Does it look good?" Shane asked, trying to peer over her shoulder.

"Yep. See, I'll be able to watch him here. I can talk to him through the speaker if anything happens. But nothing's going to go wrong. We won't be shifted for that long."

"How many minutes should we shoot for?" Shane asked.

"An hour?" she asked. She wasn't sure how long he wanted to stay shifted. She'd only met his bear a couple of times in the past during Summer Shiftfest in town.

"That would be great." He grinned. "I was a bit worried you'd only want to be out for five minutes."

"Do you think I'm a helicopter mom?" she asked, frowning.

"Not any more than any other mother. You have every right to worry about your son when it's warranted. But if you're stressed out all the time, it's not good for your body. And I want your body to stay in tip-top shape." He slid his hands across her hips and pulled her in for a kiss. "I've been wanting to do this all day. I thought your mother was never going to leave."

"Like a tornado, she blows in and blows out just as fast, wrecking as much as she can in her path." Amber scowled.

"She probably means well."

"Maybe. But she was totally rude, bringing up a potential marriage in front of Joey. He asked me about it again right before he went to sleep."

"Really?" Shane perked up.

"I told him that if we decided to get married, I'd talk to him first to make sure it was okay with him."

"What did he say to that?" he asked.

"He says he wants you to be his dad 'forever and ever'." Her heart did a little flip as she repeated Joey's exact words.

"I don't want to pressure you into anything."

"Trust me, no one will make my marriage decisions for me, but me. Ready to shift?" she asked, intentionally changing the subject.

"Sure."

After stripping, they hung their clothes over the railing on her back porch. Her teeth chattered from the cold as she summoned her bear.

The beast roared free, twisting and ripping through muscle and sinew before finally landing on all fours. She shook her entire body, loving the way her thick fur rippled down her spine. She lifted her snout to the wind and inhaled the scents of the pine forest. During summertime, wildflowers and an abundance of animals created a unique scent. In winter, most animals hibernated, leaving only the scent of the trees and the crisp freshness of newly fallen snow.

Across from her, Shane's spine elongated. His joints snapped and muscles grew. As he transformed, she looked on in awe. He was the most gorgeous man she'd ever seen. His bear was equally impressive. Its huge paws pounded into the snow as he settled.

His spring-green eyes glittered in the moonlight. When they rested on her, a ripple shook her to the core. This man was her mate. She knew it in a visceral way, as if her very DNA was reacting to his.

She couldn't understand why she'd thought anyone else could be her mate. When she'd first met her ex, he'd seemed so perfect. But she'd been terribly wrong. She'd never regret her relationship with Fred because he'd given her Joey, but she wished she'd waited until she'd felt as if the moon and stars moved through the heavens just to witness her love for her mate.

She felt that now. Totally connected to Shane in a way she'd never been with anyone else. He was her soul. Her reason for being. Her everything. And all she had to do was tell him she loved him. It's what she needed to do if she wanted to go forward with him. If she wanted to finally be with her true soulmate.

Shane's bear sauntered toward her. He nudged her flank with his nose. She took it as a signal to get running. She couldn't wait.

Racing through the woods, she burned through all the pain and anguish she'd held onto after her divorce. She released the fear that held her back from truly falling in love with Shane. And by the time she'd lost her breath and lay panting in the snow, she was ready. Ready to tell him exactly what he meant to her.

Shane dropped to her side and rolled onto his back. He looked up at the stars. When she turned her gaze toward Ursa Major, she sighed with pleasure. Being here with him was exactly where she wanted to be.

As if to confirm her realization, a shooting star streaked across the sky. Shane's bear reached for her paw. He lay his against hers and turned to brush his snout across hers. She nuzzled him back.

After lying in the snow for a few more minutes, she decided it was time to head back home. She rolled to her feet and padded over to check the baby monitor app. Joey was still lying in bed. His little chest rose and fell in a soft rhythm.

Shane shifted before she did. He stood on her back porch, watching as she shifted into her human form. Icy air licked up her spine. She grabbed her phone and the adjustable arm before running inside. Shane followed her with their clothing.

"That was so much fun," she whispered.

"I'm glad we got a chance to do it. I love seeing you like that," he said. "So wild and free."

"I don't know about that." She laughed. "I'm as free as I can be with a kid. That's something you'll have to give up too when… if…"

"I'd give up anything for you and Joey. Anything you want. Name it." Shane placed their frozen clothes in the hamper near the washing machine.

"There's nothing I want right now but to be in your arms."

"Come to bed with me," he beckoned.

They tiptoed down the hall to her bedroom. When she closed the door, Shane moved to cup her cheeks. He brushed a soft kiss across her lips. She moaned and leaned into him, savoring the warmth of him.

As he backed toward the bed, she followed. She fell into the sheets with him and let him kiss every inch of her body. By the time he moved to claim her, she was so hot and ready for him, she was afraid she'd melt.

He made love to her with slow, deep strokes. Coaxing her higher and higher, she rode waves of pleasure until they crested, and she broke against him. He followed her, filling her with the warmth of his love.

After, she snuggled into his thick arms. She lay her head in the curve between his muscular shoulder and his hard chest.

"I love you, Shane," she whispered.

He sucked in a breath before slowly releasing it.

"I love you too." He pressed his face into her hair. "I've always loved you."

"Joey loves you too," she said.

"I want to be his stepdad."

"I hate that word."

"Why?"

"Because I have a feeling you're going to be a better dad to him that his own father ever was. I should be happy about it, but it does make me a little sad," she admitted.

"Why?"

"You should have been Joey's biological father. If only I'd waited."

"Stop," Shane said softly. "Don't regret the past. It's

over. I want you to look forward to the future. With me."

"I will. And I do."

"I do, hum?" He grinned.

"Wait! Not like that. Not yet. But soon."

"Soon." He cradled her in his arms and didn't let go for the rest of the night.

18

Amber wrapped her arms around her body as Shane gave Joey a boost up onto the horse. She stood outside the ring near Shane's large red barn. The horse hadn't taken a single step yet, but she wanted to run in and save her son.

"I don't like this," she muttered.

"It's going to be fun," Shane reassured her. "Once he gets the hang of it, we'll have a heck of a time getting him to stop."

"Joey or the horse?" she asked wryly.

"Both." Shane grinned. "Trust me. I wouldn't be doing this if I didn't think it was safe. Dale is the sweetest animal on the ranch. He wouldn't hurt a fly. It's going to be okay."

She pressed her lips together and gave him a reluctant nod. If she wanted to stop being an overprotective mother, she'd have to start getting used to activities like horseback riding. She'd never done much riding herself, but if Shane and Joey both loved to do it, then she'd have to join them.

As Joey sat in the saddle Shane bought him for Christmas, Amber took a calming breath. Although it wasn't even noon yet, she wished she'd taken Shane up on his offer of a glass of wine. It would have calmed her nerves for sure. But she'd never been one to drink before lunch, and she wasn't about to start now.

She glanced at her watch. Maybe she'd have a small glass in twenty minutes when it would be after noon.

Shane repositioned Joey's feet in the stirrups, while explaining why he needed to ride with his feet pointed properly.

"...and if you turn your boots like this, you're going to hurt you knees. You'll be putting too much pressure on them. Does that make sense?"

"Yep!" Joey grinned. "See, Mom. It's not hard."

"Shane's a good teacher."

"Thank you." Shane beamed at her before turning his attention back to Joey. "Next, let's get the reins. That's how you'll steer the horse. You want to hold on to them like this." He reached up to adjust Joey's grip.

"Is this right?"

"Exactly! Good job. Now, all you have to do to get the horse moving is to give him a little nudge with your feet. Not too much. Don't kick him. Just tap your feet against his sides."

Joey gently touched his feet to the horse's barrel. The animal took a few steps forward.

"Now, just give him a little more of a tap," Shane instructed.

This time Dale kept walking. He sauntered around the edge of the ring as if he'd done it a thousand times, which was probably true. Shane was right. She was totally overreacting to the situation. Kids learned how to ride horses all the time. He'd be fine.

As she watched her son ride, she relaxed. She silently chided herself for being so afraid of letting Joey do something that would bring him so much joy. Her son's smile was as bright as the sun. A look of sheer delight settled on his face.

"Good job, honey," she encouraged as he walked past her.

Shane climbed over the ring. He stood beside her.

"Shouldn't you stay in there?" she asked.

"He'll be fine. Dale does this all the time. It's nothing new for him." Shane wrapped an arm around her shoulders. "Stop worrying so much."

"I'm trying."

"I know you are." He kissed the top of her head. "We'll give him maybe thirty minutes. He'll be sore since he's never done this before. I wouldn't want him to change his mind about riding because he went too long on his first try. It takes time to work up to longer rides."

"Thirty minutes is about all my heart can take."

"I'm thirsty. I'm going to run in and get a soda. You want anything?" Shane asked.

"What? You can't leave him in there."

"He'll be fine."

"I'll get the soda. Where is it?" she asked.

"In the fridge. I threw in some root beer and cola. There's also water in a case by the back door. It's not cold, but if we stick a few in the snow for a couple of minutes, they'll be good to go."

"I'll be right back."

As she walked into his house, she inhaled the scent of cinnamon and pine. She wasn't entirely sure where the cinnamon smell was coming from, but the pine was from a huge Christmas tree in the corner of the living room. Shane had only decorated it with a string of colorful lights. It didn't have any ornaments. She planned on asking him about that later. It seemed odd to have such a minimalist tree. But looking around the living room, it did fit his style.

A large, chocolate brown couch sat in the center of the room. In front of it was a pine coffee table with a polished finish. A single television remote rested on the table, nothing else. There were photographs of his parents on the mantle over the fireplace. But other than that, and a few lamps, the place was sparse. Still, it suited him.

She found the sodas and water. She wasn't sure who would want what, so she piled everything into her arms and carried it toward the front door. She almost dropped a can but managed to get the door open.

As she walked down the porch steps, she glanced at the ring. At first, she wasn't sure what she was looking at. Then time slowed. She felt as if she was screaming through water. The pulse of blood rushing through her ears drowned out the sound. She dropped the drinks and ran toward the ring.

Joey lay on the ground. He wailed at the top of his lungs. Shane was on the phone calling 911. She dropped to her knees in front of her baby. His arm didn't look right. He clutched it against his chest.

"I fe-fell," he choked.

"Oh my God. Honey where does it hurt?"

"My a-arm." Huge tears ran down his face.

"Yes, he's a seven-year-old boy. He was riding a horse. It startled and bucked him. I think he has a broken arm," Shane said to the 911 dispatcher.

Amber grabbed the phone from Shane.

"Move your ass!" she screamed, totally losing control. "My son's arm is probably broken."

"Is he bleeding?" the calm, male dispatcher asked.

"No. I don't know. I don't think so." She studied Joey, who hadn't stopped yelling. "Can't you hear that? He's in pain. How long will it take to get here?"

"Ma'am, we have an ambulance en route. They'll be there in less than five minutes."

"Five minutes!" Incensed, she screamed a string of expletives.

"Calm down." Shane took the phone from her. "Yes… by the barn… okay… thank you."

"Did you just tell me to calm down?" she snarled, getting right in Shane's face.

"You're scaring him." He nodded toward Joey.

"At least I didn't almost get him killed. This is unbelievable. I knew this would happen, but I let you take him anyway. You pushed me into this. You knew I thought it was too dangerous, but you kept badgering me until I gave in."

"It wasn't his fault," Joey said, sobbing out the words between cries. "The horsey got mad."

"Why did the horsey get mad?" Amber asked, dropping to her knees in front of her son.

"One of the ranch hands dropped a bale of hay. It hit a piece of tin roofing. The noise startled Dale," Shane explained calmly.

His composed demeanor was too much. He wasn't nearly as worried as he should be.

"Unbelievable," she snapped. "You don't even care. He could be dead right now, and you wouldn't even care."

"What are you talking about?" Shane demanded. "Of course I care, but hysterics aren't going to help the paramedics get here. I had to explain the situation and our location. They wouldn't be able to find us without it. If I'd totally lost it, then they wouldn't have been able to get an ambulance moving so quickly."

"You call five minutes fast? Are you fu—kidding me?" She glanced at Joey. His eyes were wide, looking from one adult to the other. "You know what. This isn't your concern anymore. I should have known I couldn't trust you with him."

"Amber, I realize you're scared right now—"

"Don't you trying to placate me," she snarled.

"Stop being mean to him," Joey sobbed.

"It's okay. Your mom is really worried about you. That's why she's mad."

"No. I'm pissed off because I knew better. I know what's best for him. You don't. You're not his parent. I am. And that won't be changing any time soon."

She turned her back on him, still seething. She was so worked up, she had a moment of dizziness. She grabbed onto the fence encircling the ring.

"Are you okay?" Shane asked. "Are you going to pass out?"

"No," she whispered.

When he tried to touch her, she jerked her shoulders away. He sighed.

A few seconds passed before a siren cut through Joey's stifled sobs. Amber whipped around and jumped over the fence. She ran, waving her arms. The ambulance driver saw her and turned toward the ring.

When they jumped out, her knees buckled in relief. One of the medics walked toward her.

"I'm fine. Help my baby!"

Shane stood next to Joey. She wanted to be there, but she couldn't get up. She couldn't move. Terror rooted her to the spot. It wasn't until they were wheeling Joey past her that she was able to get it together again.

"Wait! I'm coming too," she said.

She staggered to her feet and walked as quickly as she dared. One of the medics helped her climb into the back of the ambulance. He pulled the door closed behind her.

As they drove away, Shane walked through the snow toward them. She was so angry she could hardly see straight. This was all his fault. She never should have listened to him.

AMBER PACED the length of the hospital's waiting room. Since Huckleberry Valley only had a clinic, she'd had to ride with the paramedics all the way to Bozeman. But at least they had a lot of doctors and surgeons on staff. Still, it did little to dampen her fear.

All around her, families were gathered, waiting to hear updates about loved ones. The tension in the room was palatable. Her bear stalked back and forth in her chest. The beast wanted to roar free and go find their cub, but she didn't know where to look.

When she'd last seen her son, over an hour earlier, the nurse had been rolling him out for X-rays. She tried to get them to let her go with them, but hospital policy meant no one was allowed in imaging unless they were hospital personnel. Everyone had to wait.

They'd said it would only take an hour. She glared at the analog clock.

At the hour and ten-minute mark, she marched toward the check-in desk.

"Can I help you?" The nurse didn't even bother to look up.

"I brought my son in over an hour ago. He was supposed to get X-rays and see a doctor. He's not back yet. Where is he?"

"Last name?" she asked in an impersonal tone.

"Logan. Joey Logan," Amber ground out.

"Hum... I'm not finding—oh, there he is. Looks like he's in surgery."

"What?" she screamed. "Surgery? He broke his arm. Why is he in surgery?"

"I'll have a nurse come out and update you in a few minutes." She still hadn't looked up. Amber fought the urge to grab her by the collar of her blue scrubs and drag her over the counter.

"I need someone to come out here right now!"

"Ma'am. I'm going to need you to calm down. The ER is backed up today, and you need to wait. If you're hungry, there's a cafeteria in the basement. Follow the signs outside the elevator."

"Unbelievable!"

Amber stomped toward the chair closest to the

double doors leading into the restricted area. There was no way in hell she'd leave the area until she knew what they were doing to him. Surgery could mean anything. It could be something as simple as repairing the break. Or it could mean he had internal damage. Maybe his spleen had burst. Maybe...

She whipped open the internet app on her phone and typed in "Potential injuries after falling from a horse". The screen filled with horrifying article titles and disgusting photos of compound fractures. She knew he didn't have that type of break, because nothing was sticking out of his skin.

As she scrolled, her phone rang. Shane's name popped up on the screen. He had to be kidding. How could he possibly think she'd be able to talk to him right now?

She ignored the call. It went to voicemail. She resumed her online search. Each link gave her more and more possibilities to worry about. When she found one that mentioned paralysis, she stifled a scream. She closed the app and shoved her phone into her purse.

This was all Shane's fault. She didn't care if it was an accident. Joey should never have been on that horse in the first place. She'd been careless, listening to someone who didn't have kids. He didn't realize the constant danger they were in. An adult could fall off a horse and probably be okay, but Joey could have died.

"Oh, my God," she whispered.

What if he *was* dead? What if they just weren't telling her?

She jumped up and ran toward the nurse. Before she could reach the desk, a gray-haired doctor in blue scrubs came out of the restricted area.

"Is there an Amber Logan here?" he asked.

"Yes! Me!" She raced toward him. "Is he still alive?"

The doctor frowned and studied his tablet. "You're Amber Logan, correct?"

"Yes, please, just tell me if he's—"

"He's fine. We had to take him into surgery to patch up a deep cut on his back. Did he fall on anything sharp?"

"I—I don't know."

"He said he fell off a horse. Could he have scraped across a rock? Those can be sharp."

"I was inside when it happened. My friend was watching him."

"Well regardless, we were able to stitch together the wound. Now, that's not the bigger issue. He has a greenstick fracture."

"What's that?"

"It's somewhat common in children who break a

bone. Their bones are softer and more flexible than adult bones, so they are less likely to have a displaced or comminuted fracture."

"What's the treatment?" she asked impatiently. She didn't need the damn history of broken bones in humans, for crying out loud.

"We'll put a cast on his arm to immobilize the bone. He'll have to stay in it for four to six weeks. We'll remove it if the X-rays show that the fracture has healed properly. The good news is that he doesn't have any nerve damage. His joints didn't break either."

"When can I see him?"

"We need you to authorize pain medication. I'll straighten the fracture and get the cast put on. The nurse will call in a few days to schedule a follow-up appointment. It's very important that you go to that appointment, because we need to know for sure that the bone is healing."

"What happens if it's not?" Her stomach soured.

"It's very unlikely that will happen, so please don't worry about it right now. I'll take you in to see him, but only for a moment. We'd like to get the bone straightened as soon as possible."

"Thank you."

"It's important that he eats well as he's recovering.

No junk food. Lots of fresh vegetables and protein. He will need it to help rebuild the bone's structure."

"Okay."

"Don't worry about remembering everything I said. The information will be in the discharge papers."

"Can we go see him now?"

"Sure."

He led her through the double doors and down a sterile white hallway. After walking through a maze of corridors, she followed him into the children's wing of the hospital. Joey was in room 302.

"Mommy!" The sadness in his eyes vanished. Happiness transformed his grimace into a smile. "They said I get to pick what color cast I want. I didn't know I was going to get one. It's so cool. Last year two kids in my school had casts. One was green and it was hard to see signatures on it, but the other was pink and that was better, but I can't have pink because I'm not a girl."

"Oh, honey." She carefully navigated around the bed and leaned over to give him a soft hug. "I'm so glad you're going to be okay."

"Maybe they have yellow? It will be like sunshine on my arm. That would be awesome!"

A nurse dressed in yellow, happy face scrubs

walked into the room. "How's the best patient in the world doing?"

"Can I have a yellow one?" Joey asked.

"For your cast? Sure. We have purple, white, gray, yellow, pink, green, orange, black, and red. You can choose which ever one you want." She turned to Amber. "Are you his mother?"

"Yes."

"Great. I just need you to sign here authorizing treatment. I'll get everything ready. It shouldn't take too long."

Amber signed the paperwork then sat by her son's side and waited. True to her word, the nurse returned a few minutes later with a cart full of supplies.

As Amber watched her wrap her baby's arm, her rage toward Shane returned. He'd never be father material. He just didn't understand risk. It broke her heart to think about losing him, but her son had to come first. She didn't care if other people thought she should put herself first. She wasn't that kind of mother. And anyone who thought she was didn't know her at all.

19

Amber settled Joey into bed. After a long day at the hospital, his eyes drooped. The pain medications left him drowsy. But at least he wasn't hurting so badly anymore. The thought of her baby being in even a little pain killed her, especially since there was nothing she could do about it.

She kept his door open a crack in case he needed anything. She didn't plan on sleeping tonight. She couldn't risk not hearing him if he called for her. More than anything, he needed to know that she was there to protect him.

As she walked into the kitchen, she hung her head. She'd completely failed as a mother. She should have listened to her instincts. Letting Shane override her decision was a moment of weakness she'd never repeat. Until Joey was an adult on his own, she couldn't afford to let romance cloud her judgment.

She cared deeply for Shane, but she'd never choose him over her son. And that's what this was, a binary choice. There was no way she could love both equally. As soon as her son had been born, she'd dedicated her entire life to him. Maybe her choice had helped unravel her marriage, but there were other issues not related to their child. Eventually, even without Joey, they would have divorced.

After pouring a large glass of chardonnay, she wandered into the darkened living room and sat on the couch. The Christmas tree sat unlit in the corner. She wrapped a blanket around her body and stared into the void inside the fireplace. The urge to get up and light it came and went. She didn't have the strength. The emotional impact of the day finally hit her full on, leaving her breathless.

She slowed her breathing so she wouldn't pass out. How could she help her son if she succumbed to weakness?

Her phone sat on the coffee table. She considered calling her mother, but she didn't feel like being yelled at tonight. If her mom found out from someone else, there would be hell to pay, but Amber just didn't care. She was so sick of everyone else telling her how to live her life. She didn't need them. She didn't need anyone. And she didn't need Shane's love.

She folded her legs under her and sipped wine until the glass wouldn't give up another drop. Walking to the kitchen seemed like an impossible task, so she didn't even attempt it. Instead, she flicked on the television and turned it as low as possible. She wished she'd invested in wireless headphones so she wouldn't have to strain to hear, but it was just one more mistake she'd made.

A little after ten p.m., a soft knock sounded on her front door. She glared at it. There were only two people who would show up at her house at this hour, her mother or Shane, and she didn't want to see either. She sat totally still, willing whomever it was to go away.

The louder, second series of knocks brought her to her feet. Furious at the interruption, she stalked toward the door. She peered through the peephole. It was Shane, looking contrite as hell. He held his Stetson in his hands while he stared at the floor.

"Go away," she said as loud as she dared.

"Please let me come in and talk to you," he said.

"No. You've done enough. I don't want to speak to you right now. In fact, I don't think we'll have anything to discuss ever again."

"Don't shut me out like this."

"I can do whatever the hell I want," she snapped before lowering her voice. "Please, go away."

"Amber, I swear I'll break down this door if I have to. I need to find out how Joey's doing. The hospital wouldn't tell me a damn thing because I'm not family."

"That's right." She laughed bitterly. "You're not family. I appreciate everything you've done for me over the years, but we're done. I'll find someone else to babysit Joey. I can't trust you with him."

"It was an accident." Annoyance entered his voice.

"An accident that wouldn't have happened if I'd stood up to you. I knew it was dangerous, but I let you talk me into it anyway. I won't let you do that again."

He was silent for so long that she checked to see if he was still outside. He was. Still rooted in the same place. Still looking like he'd been kicked in the gut by a stallion. Good. He deserved it. After what he'd put her through today, he should be in pain.

"I know you're really mad right now. And probably scared," he said, finally.

"You don't know how I feel. Don't pretend to have any clue. You don't know what it was like to wait around in the hospital, wondering if your child was going to die."

"If you'd let me come with you—"

"Seriously? You think after what you did you have the right to anything?"

"You're being totally unreasonable." He raised his voice.

"If you don't leave right now, I'm calling the sheriff."

"Fine. I'll go. But this isn't over."

She fumbled with the lock then yanked open the door.

"It's over. I made a huge mistake with you. I should have trusted myself more. Bringing any man into Joey's life was a recipe for disaster. I knew it, but I let my... my..." She couldn't say desire. "Just go!"

"Please don't do this." His face hung and his eyes glinted in the moonlight. "I love you."

"Well, I don't love you. I thought I did, but I was wrong. Goodbye Shane."

She shut the door before she could get lost in his gorgeous green eyes. Even now, with anger boiling her blood, she still longed to touch him. It was ridiculous. She'd never touch him again.

She leaned her back against the door. After several minutes, his footsteps sounded down the porch steps. The door to his truck slammed shut. The engine started. He idled for another few minutes before pulling away.

Sliding to the floor, she finally gave in to the tears she'd been fighting all day. She sobbed over everything she'd lost today. How did it all change so fast? Two days ago, she'd been ready to marry him. She hadn't told him as much, but in her heart, she'd wanted to. Good thing she didn't. It would be a little easier to let him go now.

She laughed bitterly. Nothing was easy about the situation. Her traitorous heart still loved him. But she couldn't give in to those feelings. As long as she had Joey, she intended to be fully responsible for him. She'd never make the mistake of falling in love with someone ever again.

Shane's bear snarled and fought for control. The beast was furious that Shane hadn't found a way to stay with their mate. Their cub was hurt, and they couldn't even be with him. Although he'd tried to explain to his bear that they weren't the boy's father, the beast refused to accept it. As far as his bear was concerned, Joey was their son and they needed to be with him.

He managed to wrestle for domination and win long enough to get home. When he stepped out of the truck, he didn't bother trying to fight his bear any longer. The beast surged to the surface, breaking and snapping sinew and bones. Shane's clothing shredded. His boots flew off as his feet morphed into huge paws. Sharp claws dug into the frozen earth.

Inside the barn, the horses whinnied and kicked, as if sensing a nearby predator. They were right.

Shane's bear stalked toward the forest, bent on destruction. His animal was smart enough to know not to destroy any of the property on the ranch, but everything in the woods was fair game.

He crashed through snowy underbrush. Branches and brambles tore at his fur, but he welcomed the pain. Physical wounds beat emotional ones every time. He wanted to hurt. To bleed. To serve whatever penance it would take to make Amber understand that he would die for her and Joey. He'd never intended for the boy to get injured. It was an accident. Only Amber didn't see it that way. In her eyes, he'd failed her. And maybe she was right.

Suddenly, he sensed movement in the darkness. The hair on the ridge of his back stood on end. Pairs of small, chilling eyes circled him. Hiding behind bushes and trees, the wolf pack studied their prey. The alpha let out a low growl. A call to action. A call to battle.

Shane reared on his hind legs and roared. He

wasn't about to be intimidated by them. This was his damn forest.

To prove his superiority, he dropped to all fours and bounded toward the alpha. The lead wolf flexed and sprang forward, completely undaunted by the snarling bear rushing toward him.

They clashed in a tumble of snapping jaws. Knife-like claws dug into Shane's flank. Furious at the attack, he grabbed the alpha's front leg in his jaw. Before he could bite down and snap the bone, two more wolves joined the fight.

The female landed on his back. She sunk her teeth into his meaty right shoulder. Holding on as if her life depended on it, she locked her jaw, refusing to be flung free.

The beta male wrapped its mouth around Shane's rear leg. A mistake. With a swift kick, he dislodged the wolf and sent it flying. It yelped as it crashed into a nearby tree. A sickening crack sounded. The wolf went silent.

Shane redirected his attention to the alpha. It backed up several feet before charging him. This time Shane was ready. He slammed a paw into the wolf's snout. Its nose broke. Blood gushed. It howled in agony.

Only one threat remained, the female. She proved

to be a bigger issue than he'd anticipated. He swatted her with his claws, but she refused to release him. Her jaw clenched harder, sending a sharp slice of pain down his shoulder.

Using three paws, he ran as fast as he could toward the nearest tree. He slammed his shoulder into it. The wolf yipped, releasing its hold. He turned on her, going for the throat.

With that threat neutralized, he turned to find the alpha retreating with the remaining wolves. Shane snarled, watching them as they disappeared into the dark night.

Two wolves lay completely still in the clearing. He checked to make sure they were dead. He couldn't risk leaving them to attract more predators, so he used his front paws to dig graves. His shoulder ached at the site of the she-wolf's bite. He'd need to tend to it quickly to avoid infection.

After burying the wolves, he lumbered back to his house. He shifted outside, grabbed his torn clothing, and headed in. He dumped the clothes into the trash. They'd been destroyed by the shift.

In the bathroom, he thrust his shoulder toward the mirror to get a better look. Blood trickled from the bite. The edges resembled raw hamburger.

He opened the medicine cabinet and pulled out a

tube of antibiotic cream which he set on the counter. He grabbed a bottle of hydrogen peroxide and poured it over the wound. It sizzled and bubbled, burning for several seconds.

Since the bite was so deep, he took a clean washcloth and gently probed the holes to check for debris. Satisfied it was as clean as he could get it, he slathered on the cream. He finished by affixing a large bandage to his skin to cover the area.

"Stupid wolves," he growled.

After cleaning blood off the bathroom counter, he went to the kitchen to grab a beer. He plopped onto his couch. The Christmas tree was on a timer, so it twinkled with multi-colored lights. A festive reminder of everything he'd lost today.

He'd thought teaching Joey to ride would help cement Shane's relationship with Amber. Instead, it destroyed it. He never could have predicted the accident. He couldn't remember the last time he'd seen Dale buck. And then Joey had landed wrong, turning an accident into a serious medical situation.

Not being able to go to the hospital with them had nearly killed Shane. He'd tried calling several times, but the nurses wouldn't tell him anything, not even if Joey was still alive. He understood why, but it was still enraging.

As he sipped his beer, he narrowed his gaze. The lights blurred into a kaleidoscope of color. He had to find a way to fix this. There was no way in hell he was going to give up on his mate. She might be furious at him right now, but tomorrow she'd be calmer. He just had to wait until she'd gotten past the initial shock of her son's injury.

FOR THE NEXT WEEK, Shane called Amber every day. She refused to answer, so he left messages. He told her how much he loved her. He promised her he'd never do anything to put Joey in danger again. He begged and pleaded and eventually cried because he needed her. Being without her was like watching his soul slowly die. He couldn't take it.

As time went on, his patience waned. He felt terrible about what had happened to Joey, but it wasn't Shane's fault. It wasn't fair that Amber chose to blame him. She could hide all she wanted, but he wasn't going away.

He glanced at the clock on his stove. It was New Year's Eve, almost midnight. He couldn't imagine being away from her tonight. She was his mate. Not a passing fancy. Not a plaything for fun sex. No. What they shared was far deeper, and he wasn't going to let her shut him out.

He pulled his denim jacket on over his flannel shirt. He shoved his feet into his boots and tucked the hem of his jeans below the top of them. Going over there right now might be the stupidest thing he'd done so far, but he couldn't wait any longer.

As he drove toward Amber's house, he battled the voice in his head telling him this was a terrible idea. He didn't care. He couldn't mess up any worse than he'd already done.

He pulled up to her dark home. He wasn't surprised, considering the late time. Joey would be in bed. Amber would probably be sleeping too. But he needed to talk to her.

After knocking on the door several times, he sighed. He wasn't giving up, so he circled around back to Amber's bedroom window. He rapped on it twice before trying to peek through the glass.

He drew back sharply. Her bed was empty.

He raced over to Joey's window and looked in. Also empty.

Balling his fists, he shook his head. She couldn't have moved on already, could she?

No. She had to be somewhere else. Maybe her mother's house.

He sped all the way to Blythe's house. Amber's car wasn't in the driveway, but that didn't stop him from knocking on the front door.

Blythe cracked it open. She wore a bathrobe and hair rollers. The scowl on her face turned into a smile. "What are you doing here?"

"Where's Amber?"

"Well, hello to you too." She smirked, putting her hand on her hip.

"I need to talk to her."

"About damn time you did. She's still a pissed off momma bear about Joey, but she's moping around like someone died. She needs you. She just doesn't want to admit it."

"I tried to find her at home, but she's not there."

"Oh, right. Melody, Wyatt, Holly, Jace, Shannon, and that Raven girl are all celebrating together at Melody's place. They invited me, but I can't stay up this late anymore. I need my beauty rest." She patted her hair rollers before glancing at her watch. "If you can get there fast enough, you might be in time for a New Year's kiss."

Shane was already down the steps, running toward his truck.

"You can thank me later," Blythe called.

"I owe you!"

"Damn right you do!"

He took off like the devil himself was nipping at his heels. He had to get to her before midnight. Not that she was going to turn into a pumpkin or anything. But somehow, he just knew he had to get to his mate. And he was going to convince her once and for all that she belonged with him.

20

Amber couldn't wait for the clock to strike midnight. The end of this year had been a total disaster. Maybe next year would be better. Trying to get away from the raucous party, she hid in Melody's kitchen. She sipped a glass of chardonnay to calm her nerves. It wasn't working worth a damn, but maybe if she kept drinking, she'd forget her broken heart.

"There you are." Holly walked into the kitchen with an empty appetizer platter. "I thought maybe you'd escaped out the back door."

"No. I just needed a minute."

"Crazy party, hu? Melody didn't think everyone would show up. She's a bit overwhelmed. I told her I'd handle the food, so at least she doesn't have to worry about that. We went to the city and got a freezer full of appetizers. We haven't tried the little quiche yet, so I'm going to throw some in the oven."

"Quiche is nice," Amber said. She had trouble focusing on Holly, because she couldn't stop thinking about Shane. She had to stop. She was just torturing herself at this point.

"Nice. Hum." Holly side-eyed her as she took a box out of the freezer. She grabbed one of the baking trays.

As Holly arranged the small, frozen snacks, Amber struggled to come up with anything to say, so she remained silent.

"Where's Shane?" Holly asked. "I figured he'd be with you tonight."

"No idea. We broke up."

"What?" Holly whipped to look at her, eyes wide. "When did that happen?"

"The day Joey broke his arm."

"Why?" Holly opened the oven door and shoved the trays in. She set the timer.

"He's irresponsible," Amber said. "I can't trust him to be around Joey."

"But Shane's been babysitting him for years."

"I guess I was blind to the fact that I can't trust him." Amber sighed.

"What did he do? You used to count on him all the

time." Holly frowned as she leaned a hip against the counter.

"He's the reason Joey's in a cast right now. I told him horseback riding was too dangerous, but he kept talking and talking until I gave in. He convinced me it would be safe. And now look."

"Wasn't it an accident? Someone told me a bale of hay hit a tin roof piece or something," Holly said.

"Yes, but if Joey hadn't been on the horse in the first place, then he never would have gotten hurt."

"Kids get hurt all the time. It's part of being a kid, especially a boy. Jace was always falling off trees or twisting his ankle. I don't know how many times his mother had to take him in for X-rays. It's just what boys do at that age."

"Maybe his mother should have been more involved so Jace wouldn't have been hurt all the time." Amber didn't mean to sound so snappy, but anger kept her from staying calm. Why didn't anyone else understand her reasoning?

"Ha! His mom was a real bitch, still is. Back then she was even more protective of him than she is now. He was her golden boy. Keeping him out of trouble would have been an impossible task. No mother can keep an eye on her children twenty-four hours a day. It's just not possible," Holly said.

"Maybe not, but a mother should at least try to keep her kids safe. Letting Joey go horseback riding went against every instinct in my body."

"So why did you let him go?"

"Because of Shane. He talked me into it. He swore Joey wouldn't get hurt. But he did. I can't trust him anymore." Amber's belly churned. She rubbed her hand over it.

"Are you okay?" Holly asked.

"Fine."

"You're doing the preggo woman thing." Holly's gaze dropped to Amber's belly.

"I'm not pregnant." At least she didn't think she was. Wait a minute. When was her last cycle?

"You don't sound sure about it," Holly said.

"I highly doubt I am. Anyway, I don't want to talk about this anymore. Shane and I are done. Nothing he can say will change it."

"That's unfortunate."

"Why?"

"Because he seems like a good man. He's smart. He has a good job and a huge ranch. And I've seen the way he is with Joey. Shane would make a great father." Holly flicked on the oven light and leaned to check the quiche. "Needs a few more minutes."

"When Joey's an adult and he's out of the house,

then I'll think about dating. Until then, I just can't take the risk."

"What are you going to do with Joey after school? Wasn't Shane picking him up almost every day?" Holly asked.

"There's a new daycare center opening next week. I can take him there. Raven's going to be working at the bakery when we re-open. In fact, now that I think about it, she can watch him. I'll pay her. It will be a good deal for both of us while the bakery is being rebuilt. I'll only need her help a few hours a day while I check in on the construction. After we're back in business, I'll see if Raven can pick him up and take him to daycare. I'm sure I'll be fine in the bakery while she's gone. Mid-afternoons are really slow anyway."

"You'd trust random daycare workers instead of Shane?" Holly asked skeptically.

"Sure. They must be vetted or something, right?"

"Maybe. But you hear stories all the time about how some creeper got through the background check without getting flagged. If they don't check across state lines, or if they lie on their application about where they've worked in the past, then they might slip through. There are a lot of predators out there."

Amber's belly clenched.

"I'm not trying to scare you. But if I had the choice

between Shane and some random person, I'd pick Shane," Holly said.

"But he hurt Joey."

"No. He tried to teach him how to ride. He didn't knock over the hay bale, and he didn't make the horse buck. It was a freak accident. You can't blame him for that," Holly said.

"Can't blame who for what?" Melody walked into the kitchen.

"Amber blames Shane for Joey's broken arm."

"Why?" Melody frowned.

"Because I didn't want my son up on a huge horse, but I gave in to Shane."

"I tried to tell her it was an accident," Holly said, flashing a placating smile at Amber.

"Shane didn't push Joey off the horse, right?" Melody asked.

"He may as well have," Amber grumbled. They were ganging up on her, and she didn't like it one bit. "When you have kids, you can raise them however you like. But this is my son we're talking about."

"I understand the desire to protect your baby," Melody said, rubbing her stomach. "But don't you think you're taking it a bit too far? Shane's a great guy. I'd hate for you to let him get away because of this. It really wasn't malicious. He'd never do anything intentionally to hurt Joey. Anyone can see that Shane loves him. And he loves you too."

"He's called me literally every single day since the accident."

"Have you tried talking to him?" Holly asked.

"No." Amber averted her eyes so she wouldn't have to see the judgment in theirs.

"Maybe you should. He probably feels terrible about what happened. He didn't just lose Joey, he lost you too. It's so sad." Tears welled in Melody's eyes. "I'm sorry guys. It's the hormones. I cry over cereal commercials."

"I was like that with Joey too," Amber said. "It will take some time to pass, but it won't be forever. Just hang in there."

Holly wrapped an arm around Melody's shoulders. Amber wanted to hug her friend too, but she was still a bit upset at her. Probably because Holly was right. If Amber took a step back and looked at things totally rationally, she knew it was an accident. Shane wouldn't injure her son on purpose. And yet she couldn't get past the emotional side of her that still blamed him.

"The ball's going to drop in twenty minutes," someone from the party yelled. A cheer went up in the living room.

"We should get back," Melody said.

"I'll get the appetizers out of the oven in one minute." Holly nodded toward the timer which was counting down the last seconds.

"Great. How's my makeup? Did I cry it all off?" Melody asked.

"It looks perfect. Are you using the waterproof brand I told you about?" Holly asked.

"Yes! I love it. It doesn't glop up or anything."

"It's the best."

The oven beeped.

"I've got it!" Holly pulled on a pair of oven mitts.

"I should start pouring champagne for the toast," Melody said.

"Go back to the party. I'll do it," Amber said.

"Thank you so much." Melody gave her a tight hug.

After she left, Amber grabbed glasses while Holly arranged the food on the serving tray. They worked in silence until they were both ready to head back to the party.

"Think about what we told you," Holly said as she lifted the trays. "If you let Shane go, you will regret it for the rest of your life. I made that mistake once. I got lucky, because Jace came back for me. But not everyone gets a second chance."

Amber didn't respond, but she was considering her advice. She knew how much pain Holly had gone through after she lost Jace. And she knew how much joy flooded back into Holly's life when Jace returned. She was like a different person. All the bitterness she'd carried for years was gone now. Holly walked around with a smile on her face ninety percent of the time, which was a huge improvement to her perpetual, pre-Jace scowl.

She'd have to think about what they'd said a bit more. Maybe they were right. Kids did get hurt no matter what someone did to protect them. She couldn't expect Joey to sit at home and avoid anything potentially dangerous. He'd end up resenting her for it.

The laughter and chatter in the living room reached a fever pitch. She gathered the champagne glass stems between her fingers and wrapped her arms around two champagne bottles.

As she started toward the kitchen door, it opened. She froze, nearly dropping all the glasses.

"Shane! What are you doing here?"

"We need to talk." He gently took the flutes from her fingers and set them to the side. "Right now."

Shane's bear paced back and forth in his chest, silently warning him not to screw things up. Trying to convince his mate that they belonged together would be the most important conversation of his life. And yet, he had no idea how to start.

"How did you get in?" Amber asked.

"I knocked until someone opened the door."

"How did you find me?"

"Your mother."

"My mother?" Amber brought her hand to her throat. "How did you convince her to tell you where I was tonight?"

He knew she was asking pointless questions just to stall, but he didn't care. He still hadn't come up with a good way to tell her how much he loved her. But he had to, even if it didn't come out perfect.

"Amber, I need to tell you—"

"Hey, Shane." Wyatt strolled into the kitchen. "Didn't know you were here."

"Just got here."

"Cool. Melody needs the champagne glasses."

"I was about to bring them out," Amber said.

"I've got it." Wyatt picked up everything she'd been carrying. "See you in a few minutes. The ball's about to drop."

"But we're on Mountain time." Amber shot Wyatt a questioning look.

"I don't know. It's pre-recorded or something. Time zones suck." Wyatt grinned before leaving the room.

"We should go out—"

"Wait!" Shane gently grabbed her wrist. "What I need to say will only take a minute."

"We only have a few." She glanced at her watch.

"I'll be fast." He cleared his throat and ignored his pounding heart. "I feel terrible about what happened to Joey. It nearly killed me when I saw him fall. But it was an accident."

"I know," she said softly.

"Really? Because you sure haven't been acting like it. You've been blaming me."

"Well, I was wrong." She crossed her arms over her chest.

"Um..." He rubbed the back of his neck. "Okay."

"I was mad."

"And scared, too?" he asked.

"Very." She shivered.

"Honey, life is always going to be risky. It's messy around the edges. And even if we try like hell to keep Joey safe, he might still get hurt."

"I know. I hate it, but I get it. I'm sorry I yelled at

you and didn't return your calls. I should have at least talked it over with you. That was my mistake."

"It's okay," he said.

"No. It's not. I treated you like you were a monster, and you're anything but."

"So you forgive me?"

"There's nothing to forgive. If anything, I should be asking you to forgive me for being such a crazy person." She sighed and leaned against the kitchen counter.

"Well, I'm waiting." He smiled, hoping to add some levity to the tense situation.

"Shane, I was a total jerk. I was mean and rude, and if you don't want to have anything to do with me—"

"I love you! God, Amber. Don't you get it? I've always loved you. I get why you were mad, and I'm not entirely happy you took it out on me, but I understand why it happened that way. I don't care about that anymore. I love you, and I can't live without you."

"Shane," she whispered.

He pulled her into his arms and rested his chin on the top of her head. He held her until she released him.

"How can you still love me after how mean I was to you?" she asked.

"Because you're my mate. We belong together. When we met, I felt a connection unlike anything I've ever experienced. You were different, but I wasn't sure how. I figured it was just because you were such a good friend. My bear tried to convince me we were destined to be together, but I didn't think I deserved it."

"Why not?"

"I did something years ago that I deeply regret." He sighed, knowing he needed to tell her the truth about the pain he'd been holding onto. "When I was a teenager, I convinced my friends to go rock climbing in a remote area. One of the guys wasn't the best climber, but I talked him into going anyway. He fell."

"Oh, no."

"Search and rescue couldn't get a helicopter to our location. There was nowhere to land, and by the time they hiked in..." His voice broke.

"He didn't make it," Amber finished.

"No. Because of me."

"It wasn't your fault, Shane. It was an accident."

"And I see that now because of what happened with Joey. When he got hurt, it was also just a freak accident. I didn't cause it. That damn ranch hand with the hay bale caused it. And I didn't cause my friend's death either. He's the reason I got into EMS, and he's why I haven't been able to bring myself to leave. But now I can."

"Because you see that it wasn't your fault," she said softly. "Oh, Shane. I had no idea."

"Of course not. I never told you." The corner of his mouth quirked. "But we have to stop doing that. If there's something we need to figure out, we have to talk about it. We might argue and disagree about things sometimes, but we can't do what we've been doing the last few days. We can't ignore each other."

"I was the one doing the ignoring," she admitted. "Not you."

"Yes. But my point is that we can't shut each other out. If I'm going be Joey's stepdad, then we're going to have to make a lot of decisions together. It can't just be you making choices for us all the time."

"I know, but I'm always so afraid of making a mistake."

"You're part human. As shifters, we'll always make mistakes because we're trying to live complicated lives. There are a million choices to make every day. Sometimes, we're going to screw up. But we can't ever lose sight of one thing."

"What's that?" she asked.

"Our love. You're everything I've ever wanted in a

mate. More than I ever dared to dream about. I want to be with you for the rest of our lives. If you'll have me."

"Shane!" She flung herself into his arms.

He clung to her, unwilling to let go for even a second. He could hardly catch his breath, but it didn't matter. She was his. Now and forever.

"Mommy! The ball's falling down! Hurry!" Joey ran into the kitchen and out of it just as quickly.

"Well, we can't miss the ball, can we?" Shane asked in a naughty tone.

"You're terrible," she said before grabbing his hand and leading him back to the party.

Amber handed them each a glass of champagne. The count started.

"Ten, nine, eight, seven, six, five, four, three, two, one, Happy New Year!"

Shane clinked his glass against Amber's and downed it as fast as he could. He set it on a side table and grabbed her glass when she finished it. He pulled her close and forgot about everyone else in the room. It was just him and his mate. And he wanted to start this year, and every year after it, with her in his arms.

He kissed her with all the passion he'd kept trapped in his heart his whole life. She melted against him, tangling her fingers into his hair and pressing against him until he was hard and breathless.

When he finally broke the kiss and stepped back, he realized all eyes were on them. Applause broke out.

"Damn, honey," Holly said to Jace. "I'm going to need you to kiss me like that later."

"Why don't I do it right now?" Jace grabbed his fiancée and yanked her into his lap. He kissed her while everyone chuckled.

"Mommy!" Joey ran up to her and Shane. "Does this mean Shane's going to be my daddy?"

Shane squatted until he was eye level with the boy. "Would you like that?"

"Yay! I have a real daddy now!" Joey threw his good arm around Shane.

"He's been asking if you're coming over to sign his cast," Amber said.

"Anyone have a pen?" Shane asked.

"I've got a Sharpie collection," Melody said with a laugh.

"She's already into baby scrapbooking, and our kid isn't even here yet." Wyatt wrapped his arms around his wife.

"She or he will be here soon enough," Melody said. She returned a minute later with a variety of colors.

"You pick," Shane told Joey.

"How about..." Joey stared intently at the selection. "That one!"

"Where should I sign?" Shane asked, grabbing the blue marker.

"Right in the middle." Joey held out the arm with the yellow cast.

"Yellow and blue make green," he said as he signed the cast.

"It's so cool. They said I can put stickers on it too."

"We'll get you a bunch of stickers," Shane said.

He looked up to see Amber discreetly wiping tears from her eyes. His heart swelled with love. He planned on making her as happy as he possibly could for the rest of their lives. It was a New Year's resolution he intended to keep.

21

Three months later, Amber stared out her kitchen window. As the sun rose, snow melted and dripped off the roof. Tulips bloomed alongside the road. Daffodils turned their yellow faces toward the warmth. Birds chirped and flitted through the air. The first signs of spring brought a smile to her face. Gratitude flowed out from her heart to bathe her in the warm glow of satisfaction.

Today was the grand opening of her new bakery. She'd spent the last week frantically getting ready for the rush of customers she anticipated. Almost everyone in Huckleberry Valley had stopped by during construction to let her know they couldn't wait for the re-opening. She was just as eager to get back into a routine.

Shane padded out from the hall. His loose flannel pajama pants hung low enough to make her mouth water. She dragged her gaze up to meet his. He grinned and walked her back against the counter. He leaned his palms against it, caging her between his arms. A shiver of desire shimmied through her core.

"I'm sure we could fit a quickie in before we go," he murmured, kissing her neck.

"You know I want to, but there's so much to do."

"They can wait." He tugged at the tie on her robe.

"You're so terrible," she moaned as he nibbled her earlobe.

"The worst."

"Pure evil."

"And you love it."

"I do." She wrapped her arms around his neck. "We don't have time, but we will later. Do you think you can hold that thought for a few hours?"

"Sweetie, you'll be naked in my mind all day."

She laughed. A lightness filled her chest. She'd spent every day with Shane since New Year's. They were planning on moving into his place later in the springtime. She'd sell her house when it was warmer and there were more buyers looking for places.

"I have to get dressed. We prepped a lot of the

dough last night, but I still need to bake everything. And I need to get Joey ready."

"Go on ahead while I get him dressed. I'll make sure he has breakfast before we go to the bakery."

"You're so good to him."

"He's my boy, and I love him. I think I'll make cinnamon apple pancakes today."

"You're turning into quite the gourmet chef. I might have to drag you into the kitchen as soon as you arrive."

"I'll help any way I can, even if it's just doing dishes. Today's going to be amazing." He kissed her softly. "Go on, honey. I don't want you stressing today. It's going to be a great start to the next phase of your goals."

"I already have everything I could ever want," she said.

"Well, there are always bigger ovens out there," he teased.

"True." She tapped her finger on her chin. "And if you're willing to work for free…"

"Oh, boy. Maybe I should have kept my mouth shut. I don't want to end up sweating over a hot oven all day." He grinned.

"Nope. You'll end up chasing around a seven-year-old. That's much harder than standing around in a kitchen. Good luck." She rubbed her nose against his. "See you in an hour or so."

"I'm already looking forward to it." He gave her butt a pat as she walked past.

After getting dressed in a comfortable pair of black yoga pants and a red tunic sweater, she drove to the new bakery. She'd been able to purchase the old laundry space which had also burned down in the fire. The owner had chosen to retire and was happy to sell to Amber.

With all the extra space, she was able to expand the kitchen section of the bakery, as well as add additional seating. She wanted to keep the aesthetic of the original shop, so she went with white Formica countertops, a pink and white checkered floor, and cotton candy pink, gumdrop-shaped stools along the much longer lunch counter. Shane had scrunched his nose at all the pink, but she didn't care. She loved it.

As she unlocked the back door, the scent of cinnamon and star anise hit her nose. She found Raven in the kitchen already mixing a huge batch of dough for cinnamon rolls. Additional ingredients for the cream cheese frosting sat on the large, stainless-steel prep table.

"I'm so excited about today," Raven said. "I can't even imagine how you feel."

"I'm about to crawl right out of my boots. Everything has to go well today."

"It will."

"You're here early," Amber said.

"I wanted to surprise you. This is your day, and you shouldn't have to work too hard. I got as much done as I could in the last hour, but we still need to make all the croissants and most of the other pastries."

"I'm on it."

They worked quickly, mixing and kneading dough. They shoved tray after tray into the huge ovens, pulling out scrumptious treats from previous batches to make room. By the time Amber looked at the clock again, it was three minutes until their official opening time.

"Have you looked up front to see if anyone's outside?" Amber asked.

"Not yet. I'm afraid to look. I think we're about to get inundated with guests. Not that it's a bad thing, but I don't know if I've had enough coffee yet."

"We have two minutes to fix that." Amber quickly poured two cups of coffee. She handed one to Raven then held hers up in a toast. "To the future of the bakery!"

"To the future!" Raven smiled before lightly

tapping her mug against Amber's. She downed the whole thing in one long chug. "Let's do this!"

When Amber walked into the main dining area, her heart stopped. Through the glass windows along the entire front wall, dozens of smiling faces greeted her. Everyone in town had to be standing outside, waiting for a seat.

"Oh, crap!" Raven laughed as she walked up next to Amber. "We might need a few shots of espresso instead."

"Hopefully they don't stampede," Amber said, chuckling nervously.

As she unlocked the front door, two of her favorite older customers grinned. They were always her first guests, and today was no exception. They were first in line.

"Mornin' Amber," Old Man Walters said. "You still getting the morning paper?"

"Every day. I've got them stacked on the counter."

"Good to see you didn't change much." He leaned in closer. "Don't let the rest of these kooks know or I'll never hear the end of it, but I'm partial to the pink. And those gumdrop seats. Reminds me of playing Candyland as a boy."

"I won't tell a soul." She grinned as he walked past.

"Save me a seat," his friend Paul hollered.

Amber tried not to laugh, because they were the first two people to step inside. There were plenty of seats.

After letting in as many people as the fire regulations allowed, Amber went to work. As she took orders, she accepted compliments from guests who loved that she'd kept the old style. Things tended to move slowly in Huckleberry Valley, and everyone wanted it to stay just the way it was. She completely agreed.

Back in the kitchen, Raven worked like a maniac to fill the first rush of orders. She helped Amber carry plates out before returning with a coffee pot in each hand to provide refills. Despite the rush and subsequently slow service, no one complained. They seemed content enough to enjoy being back at Sweet Cheeks.

The initial rush never died down. A line went out the door until well after noon. Shane and Joey had arrived a bit earlier. They were helping Raven in the kitchen. Under Shane's supervision, Joey added ingredients to the mixing bowls. He got to press the button to start the mixers, but Shane watched him like a hawk to make sure he wouldn't get hurt again. Amber completely trusted him.

"Is it still crazy out there?" Shane asked.

"I thought it would calm down after the lunch rush, but it's still nuts. Thank God we ordered extra butter," Amber said.

"Only a few hours left." Shane kissed her cheek. "We're almost there. Tonight, you'll get the best foot rub ever."

"You're so sweet, but I'd settle for a nap." Amber chuckled.

"A nap or a 'nap'?" Shane finger quoted.

"You're so bad." Amber shook her head. Before she walked back into the dining room, she cast a look over her shoulder. "I'll take both."

"I knew it!" he yelled.

She giggled as she went to take more orders.

The rest of the afternoon was a blur, and by five p.m. she was dead on her feet. Her heels throbbed, and her neck ached. She rubbed the back of it as she locked the front door.

"We made it!" Raven said as she wiped down the lunch counter area.

"Sit down, honey," Shane said to Amber. "I'll mop while Raven finishes with the tabletops."

He didn't have to ask twice. She plopped into the closest booth. Her feet throbbed. She was seriously out of practice, but being off work for almost four months would do that. She wasn't surprised.

"Mommy?" Joey ran over from the booth where he'd been coloring in a cartoon book.

"What's up, honey?"

"Can we go to the café for dinner?" His eyes widened in anticipation.

"Oh, no," Shane said. "I've got something special planned. We're going to my house after. Raven, you're welcome to join us."

"Oh, I'd love to, but my feet are killing me too. I've got a date with the fabulous bathtub in my room at Shannon's. I still can't believe I live there."

"How has that been going?" Amber asked.

"Great! Things were hard for me for a while, but it's starting to look up, thanks to you. I'm glad you took a chance on me. I really needed it," Raven said.

"You've been doing a great job. I'm happy you're working with me. See you tomorrow?"

"Absolutely! Only tomorrow, I plan on running the espresso machine for a while, so I'm sufficiently caffeinated before the rush." Raven smiled.

"Sounds like a good plan to me," Amber said.

After Raven finished the counters and Shane washed the floor until it sparkled, she was half asleep and more than ready to lay down for a few minutes.

Fortunately, Shane suggested she do exactly that as soon as they arrived at his place. She lay on his couch while Joey played with toys in front of the fireplace.

"Babe?" Shane gently shook her awake.

"Oh, wow. Did I fall asleep?" She blinked up at him.

"Only for a few minutes. Dinner's ready."

Joey was already sitting at the table when she sat in the chair next to him.

"I helped make it," Joey said, beaming.

"Make dinner?"

"Yep. Lasagna," Joey said.

"My favorite!"

"You deserve it." Shane set the bubbling tray of lasagna on the table. "We made garlic bread too."

"You spoil me."

"Because I love you." Shane kissed her sweetly.

Later that night, Amber crawled into bed next to him. She was too tired to even consider making love. Shane must have sensed it, because he scooted down to the end of the bed and reached under the covers. As he massaged her feet, she moaned.

"Not quite how I expected to get you moaning tonight, but I'll take it," Shane joked.

"I'm sorry. I'm just so tired."

"Lay back and rest. You've got to do it all again tomorrow."

"Don't remind me," she groaned.

"Should I bring Joey again, or do you want us to stay home out of the way?"

"Either way is good. I don't think we'll be as crazy busy tomorrow."

"Joey's been asking me to let him ride Dale again," Shane said softly. "I wanted to check with you first."

She hesitated as old fears resurfaced. Joey's cast had come off a month after it went on. His arm was as good as new but having him ride again made her nervous. However, she couldn't keep him stuck inside forever.

"How about this; we'll all ride together after I get home tomorrow," she said.

"That would be awesome."

Shane's smile awakened her senses. She instantly forgot she was tired. As she pulled her legs up, Shane's eyes clouded with desire.

"I thought you were too tired," he whispered.

"I'm never too tired for you."

She reached for him, and he spent the rest of the night showing her exactly how much he loved her.

THE NEXT DAY, the bakery was just as busy as opening day. Amber didn't even notice. She was floating with happiness. She'd finally gotten everything she'd ever wanted in a bakery. It was a dream come true. She couldn't have been any happier when she finally left work.

On the drive to Shane's house, butterflies danced in her belly. She'd had perfectly rational internal debates with herself all day. Her bear had laughed at her for being so worried about Joey going riding again. Kids fell. They got hurt. It was normal. She'd repeated it until she actually believed it. But it didn't stop the nerves in her belly. Maybe she'd always be this way when it came to Joey. Maybe she'd just have to accept the primitive fear that came with motherhood.

When she reached the house, she found Shane and Joey in the stable. They'd already saddled up Dale and were walking him out.

"Hey, honey." Shane kissed her. "How was your day?"

"Wild, but we made it. If things keep going this way, I might have to hire a second employee."

"We can afford it. You should start looking," Shane said.

"Maybe when it's a little calmer and I have more time."

"Mommy, I put my helmet on all by myself!" He patted the hard-plastic helmet.

"What happened to your cowboy hat?" she asked.

"I thought this might make you feel better," Shane said.

"It does. Thank you."

"Do I look funny?" Joey asked.

"No, you look adorable," Amber said.

After getting a boost up, Joey settled into the saddle. He'd completely recovered from his injuries so his doctor said it was okay to ride, otherwise she wouldn't have considered it.

"Are you doing okay?" Shane asked.

"Yep!"

"Kids are so resilient." Shane climbed out of the ring. He stood next to her and looped an arm around her waist. After Joey went a few laps, Shane gave her a squeeze.

"Oh, no! Mommy!" Joey gasped.

"What? What's wrong?" She was halfway through the corral bars before she'd finished the question. She hurried over to where the horse stood.

"There's something stuck on the front of the saddle," Joey said.

"What?" She stood on tiptoes, trying to look. She was vaguely aware of Shane suddenly beside her.

"Here it is," Shane said. He pulled a small, black ribbon. Something fell off into his palm. He turned to her and got down on one knee.

"What is it?" she asked, trying to see what he held in his hand.

"Amber, I love you more than I've ever thought I could love another person. I knew you were destined to be my mate, but I didn't know how to make it happen. I'm glad I finally did."

Totally confused, she couldn't figure out why he was on one knee holding whatever had been tied to the horse. It didn't make any sense until he opened his palm. A white gold ring glittered in the afternoon sunlight. A sparkling round diamond sat in the center of the solitaire.

"Shane!" She looked from him to the ring and back. "You almost gave me a damn heart attack."

"I thought it would be cute."

"It's... Oh, my God. Is that..." She pressed her hand to her throat. Her heartbeat thudded against her fingers.

"Marry me," he said. "Be my mate forever. Be my wife and make me the happiest man in the whole universe."

"The whole universe?" She tried to use a playful

tone, but it came out a whisper. She was still too shocked by his surprise proposal.

"Will you marry me?" He gazed up at her, letting all the love he had for her shine brightly in his smile.

"Yes."

"Yay!" Joey screamed. "You're my new daddy for real now!"

Amber's eyes watered as she nodded at her son. She'd finally found a man who would love him as much as she did. She had absolute faith in Shane's ability to be the best father ever.

Her bear smirked and pranced around in her chest as if to say, "Told you so."

She ignored the smug beast. Her hand trembled as Shane slipped the ring onto her finger. She couldn't believe she was finally going to marry her best friend, who also happened to be the man of her dreams. She'd never thought she'd find happiness. But in his arms, she found the kind of magic that only came along once in a lifetime.

He truly was her perfect mate.

To be the first to find out about Liv's next book, and to get special offers and discounts, sign up for Liv's newsletter!

Don't miss the **Curvy Bear Ranch Series.**

Find out more about Liv on her website!

ABOUT THE AUTHOR

USA Today bestselling author Liv Brywood writes paranormal romance. Her scorching hot shifters love curvy women and aren't afraid to show it. They're loyal, brave, honorable, and above all — sexy. Liv's stories are filled with passion, hope, and everlasting love.

To be the first to find out about the next book in the series, and to get special offers and discounts, sign up for my email newsletter!

To find out more about me, please check out my website.

Friend me on Facebook.

Follow me on Twitter.

Email me at LivBrywood@gmail.com

Manufactured by Amazon.ca
Bolton, ON